Praise for *Cross My Heart,*
THE HIDDEN DIARY, book 1

Cross My Heart was *very* descriptive (but not, like, overloaded!) and fun. It's a touching story that a lot of girls can relate to because of their own busy parents. I liked the mystery, too!

> Lilly, eleven years old, daughter of Liz Curtis Higgs,
> author of *Bad Girls of the Bible*

Mama mia! *Cross My Heart* was a great book! I liked the way the author left you hanging at the end of each chapter. It made you want to keep reading. I could really relate to some of the characters, and Claudette made me laugh. You'll love this book! Cross my heart!

> Tavia, ten years old, daughter of Deborah Raney,
> author of *A Vow to Cherish* and *Beneath a Southern Sky*

This book was really good, interesting, and fun. I couldn't say I had one favorite part because I loved the whole book! I couldn't put it down.

> Tyler, eleven years old, daughter of Lisa E. Samson,
> author of *The Church Ladies*

I couldn't put this book down! I guarantee you'll love *Cross My Heart,* and it will keep you on the edge of your seat.

> Marie, thirteen years old, daughter of Terri Blackstock,
> author of the NEWPOINTE 911 series

Cross My Heart is a very exciting book. Lucy . . . meets new friends and learns about God. I know my friends will love this book like I did. Maybe we'll find a hidden diary somewhere, too.

> Madelyn, nine years old, daughter of Cindy McCormick
> Martinusen, author of *Wi*

I think Lucy and Serena are reall
HIDDEN DIARY book.

> Bethany, nine years old,
> author of *PrayerWalk* & *G*

D1516650

Books by
Sandra Byrd
FROM BETHANY HOUSE PUBLISHERS

THE
HIDDEN
DIARY

5

Pass It On

SANDRA BYRD

BETHANYHOUSE

MINNEAPOLIS, MINNESOTA

Pass It On
Copyright © 2002
Sandra Byrd

Cover illustration by Bill Graf
Cover design by Lookout Design Group, Inc.

Unless otherwise identified, Scripture quotations are from the *Holy Bible*, New Living Translation, copyright © 1996. Used by permission of Tyndale House Publishers, Inc., Wheaton, Illinois 60189. All rights reserved.

All rights reserved. No part of this publication may be reproduced, stored in a retrieval system, or transmitted in any form or by any means—electronic, mechanical, photocopying, recording, or otherwise—without the prior written permission of the publisher and copyright owners.

Published by Bethany House Publishers
A Ministry of Bethany Fellowship International
11400 Hampshire Avenue South
Bloomington, Minnesota 55438
www.bethanyhouse.com

Printed in the United States of America by
Bethany Press International, Bloomington, Minnesota 55438

Library of Congress Cataloging-in-Publication Data

Byrd, Sandra.
    Pass it on / by Sandra Byrd.
        p.   cm. — (The hidden diary ; bk. 5)
Summary: Lucy and Serena decide to do secret good deeds, and in the process, Lucy learns the difference between luck and blessings.
    ISBN 0-7642-2484-0 (pbk.)
    [1. Christian life—Fiction. 2. Friendship—Fiction. 3. Luck—Fiction.
4. Santa Catalina Island (Calif.)—Fiction.] I. Title.
    PZ7.B9898 Pas   2002
    [Fic]—dc21   2002002710

In honor and in memory of
Margaret Jenny Evanson Michelizzi,
better known as my wonderful Grandma Gussie

Contents

An Urgent Letter

Saturday afternoon . . . . D Day minus six

After a quick walk down a steamy street, Lucy Larson stepped into the Avalon post office. The air inside, like everywhere on Catalina Island, smelled of salt and sand and faintly of clams.

The chunky key slipped into the post-office box and Lucy twisted. Reaching her hand in, she grabbed the cache of letters and fished them out. A few cards, some bills forwarded from their house in Seattle . . .

Then, just as Lucy was about to stuff all the mail into her straw beach bag, she read the face of the last letter. It was addressed to her—Lucy Larson! On the edge of the letter someone had scrawled big red letters. It read, *Urgent! Open Right Away!* The return address indicated the letter was from Lucy's cousin Katie.

Katie never, ever sent real letters. Only email.

Lucy was about to rip the letter open when someone tapped her on the shoulder.

"Hi, Lucy!" came a quiet voice from behind her.

Lucy turned. "Hi, Jenny. How are you?" Jenny was twelve, same as Lucy. In fact, they'd both celebrated their birthdays just a few weeks earlier. Jenny's short brown hair was tucked behind her ears.

"Okay." Quiet Jenny seemed uncomfortable to have started the conversation. "I'm walking to the beach. Are you heading that way?"

Lucy nodded. "I'm meeting Serena there in a few minutes."

"Do you want to go together?"

Lucy smiled and closed the P.O. Box door. Jenny stood next to her, her eyes staring at the red words, *Urgent! Open Right Away!*

If I saw a letter like that, I'd probably wonder, too. Lucy reluctantly slipped the letter into her beach bag with the other mail. No telling what was in an urgent letter. It might be something she'd better read alone.

The two of them wove their way through the tourists swarming the street, toward the beach.

"I'm glad you're here this summer," Jenny said.

"Me too. At first I didn't know if I was going to spend all summer doing plant research with my dad, but it's been fun." *And if I hadn't come, I wouldn't be on my way to read an exciting old diary with Serena, my new best friend!* "Great earrings." Lucy pointed at the turquoise studs in Jenny's earlobes.

"Funny you would say that. I was just thinking that I *love* your ring." Jenny, braver now, touched the silver and turquoise ring on Lucy's hand.

"Thanks. I got it at the Navajo Nation. We visited there one year, and I met the lady who made it. She melted her own silver and smoothed her own stones and everything."

Jenny grinned. "Indian stuff is cool."

A few minutes later they arrived at the beach. Lucy reached for the sunglasses on top of her head and flipped them down over her eyes. Her pink limbs stood out like crab legs compared to all the penny-colored skin at the beach. She sighed. That was just part of being a strawberry blonde.

"Would you like to go snorkeling with us?" Jenny asked.

"Thanks for the invite, but I'm supposed to meet Serena." Lucy scanned the area. The beach glistened like cinnamon sugar on warm toast. Peeking over Jenny's shoulder, Lucy spotted Serena struggling down the beach with her big yellow umbrella. "There she is! I'd better go and help out."

Jenny nodded. "See you later."

Lucy smiled at her and raced to meet Serena. She grabbed Serena's elbow and whispered, "Let's go! Head over this way so we can have some privacy."

Normally it was fun to be in a group. But not when they read the hidden diary.

The hidden diary was for them alone.

Lucy took the umbrella from Serena. "Thanks. It was getting kind of heavy." Serena's long dark hair was French-braided and then twisted. Serena always looked so, well . . . put together.

Lucy's fuzzy hair fluffed in the surf wind.

They found a place away from the others to settle, a little patch of sand all to themselves. Serena spread out the blanket.

"I can't stay long," Lucy said. "I promised to do some chores."

"Okay," Serena said. "I'm supposed to help Roberto's *abuela* cook something today." She snorted.

"Ah." Lucy held back a smile. Roberto was Serena's half brother. "Is the bossy grandmother still making life difficult?"

Serena nodded. "Did you bring the diary?" The old diary had been written in 1932 by Serena's great-grandmother, also named Serena, and her best friend, Mary.

"Mama mia, would I forget something like that?" Lucy pulled stuff out of her bag, searching for the old diary. It had been her week to keep it.

First came the keys, then the sunscreen. Lucy pulled the mail out, too, as she dug deeper into the bag.

"What's this?" Serena asked. She pointed to the urgent letter.

"I don't know yet," Lucy answered. Serena was her Faithful Friend, but out of loyalty to Katie, Lucy felt she ought to open the letter alone. It was the right thing to do.

Lucy located the thin red diary and the key and set them like a feast of fun before her best friend. "Want to open it?"

"Okay." Serena found the fourth section and began reading.

"Oh, Diary. Problems! All the girls were over at

Trudy's house helping her do chores so she could come to the beach. Then a vase fell and broke into a hundred pieces! No one knew who had bumped it—the ones dusting or the ones sweeping or if someone else had moved it while they cleaned the mirror. The vase was old and can't be replaced. Everyone blamed someone else, and before you knew it we were all cross with one another. Worst of all, no one wanted to go to the beach together afterward. Except for the two of us, we girls haven't talked with one another since. Why did something bad happen when we were trying to do something good?'"

Serena handed the diary over to Lucy, who always read the parts that Mary had written.

" 'So, Diary,' " Lucy read.

"We decided we'll each give a small gift to at least one girl in our group—something just perfect for her—to build our friendships again. And then maybe once she gets the gift, she'll do the same for one of the other girls! Only, the gifts must stay a secret! Positively no one can know. If anyone finds out we started sending gifts, they'll think _we_ broke the vase and denied it. Which we didn't."

The writing changed back to the blocky writing, and

Lucy handed the diary back to Serena to read.

"We'll put a note with each one, telling them to keep the gifts a secret and pass on a secret gift, too. We plan to put a little rose with each gift. When they each get a rose, they'll know it's from our group, because we've called ourselves the Rose Girls. Mary and I won't give a gift to each other, of course, because we're in this together. Oolie droolie! We'll be back later to tell you if the vase breaker confesses—and if our gal pals are friends again or if we're busted up for good. Till then, Diary.

Mary and Serena,
Faithful Friends."

Serena closed the diary. "Aha! This sounds like fun."

"We each give one person a secret gift, but we can't tell anyone else," Lucy agreed. They shook hands on the deal.

Lucy squeezed Serena's hand for a moment after they shook. "I hope nothing bad happens to us, too, like it did to the diary girls when they were trying to do something good."

"We don't have any old vases," Serena tried to joke, but her voice wavered.

"I know. But I mean *nothing* bad. Not just a vase breaking."

"Um. Yeah. Me too."

Each week, Lucy and Serena copied the adventure from the old diary—doing something like the diary girls had done. It had to be done by the end of the week, Friday.

Friday was D Day, the day by which the Diary Deed had to be done and *all* was revealed.

"I don't know about the roses," Serena said. "They're pretty expensive."

Lucy thought for a moment and then suggested, "How about jasmine? We have a bush in our backyard."

"And we have a vine on the side of our house," Serena said. "It's everywhere on the Island. Jasmine it is—we put a little jasmine blossom with our gift."

"Let's not tell each other what we gave or to whom till we meet again on Diary Day," Lucy said. "A double secret." Lucy started to pack up her gear. "My mom says she has a surprise planned—including you. She's called your mom. Do you know what it is?"

"No." Serena folded the beach blanket into a neat rectangle and then into a small square before putting it away.

"I'll call you." Lucy picked up her beach bag and headed home quickly. She didn't want to rush away, but there was that letter. . . .

On the way home she slit the envelope open, not able to wait another minute.

Lucy read the letter's contents.

> *Urgent! Whoever sent this letter to you wants you to have good luck! In fact, it has been proven by hundreds of people that this letter will absolutely work. Why else would someone who cared about you send it to you? Here's what you* must *do. Send this letter to five people within two days of getting it. If you do, you will have* good *luck for five days—one day for each person you send it to, with the* best *luck happening on the last day. We promise!*

Jason in Louisiana won a cruise. Missy in Illinois found a $100 check addressed to her in her mailbox.

The last sentences were written in bold black. Lucy's heart thumped as she read the letter's ending threat.

If you don't send this letter to five people within two days, you will be responsible for breaking the chain that all the other people have worked to build. Because of that, there will be consequences. Bad luck will come your way for five days, with the worst happening on the last day. Do the right thing and get the rewards—pass this letter on now. Or else!

Man, Lucy thought. *Now what am I going to do?*

2

A Little Trip

Saturday evening . . .

It's not that chicken curry on rice isn't nice, Lucy thought later at dinner. *It's just that I want to get back and see if I can make a decision about that letter!*

But she knew her dad had worked hard cooking the meal. It had taken him a lot of time to sliver almonds, chop vegetables into tiny dice all the same size, and plump the raisins in orange juice. And curry was one of Lucy's favorites. After dinner she would go back upstairs and decide what to do.

"Well, I should have some information about our surprise after dinner!" her mother announced.

"Cool, Mom," Lucy said. Mom seemed so . . . well, emotional about this surprise. What was going on?

Lucy let her mind wander outside the conversations about bills to pay and people to call and a problem with the kitchen sink not draining right. But she leaped right in when she heard the word *China*.

"When will they leave?" Mom asked.

"On Wednesday morning," Dad answered. "They fly to China Wednesday evening from Los Angeles."

"China?" Lucy asked. "Are you talking about Claudette?"

"Yes," her dad answered. "The Kingsleys are going to pick up their new baby. Of all the summers we have worked together, this one is the most exciting."

"Oh . . . yeah." Lucy set her fork down. Claudette's family had come to Catalina Island this summer, too. Lucy baby-sat Claudette, who was sometimes annoying. But like some of the vines their fathers studied, Claudette had wrapped her way around Lucy's heart.

"Claudette will have a sister then. Right?"

"Right," her mother answered. "Isn't that nice?"

Lucy nodded, not sure why she felt sad when something good was happening to Claudette.

Suddenly the yellow curry sauce and rice tasted gluey. Lucy pushed the plate away. "Am I still going to Claudette's house while you guys, um. . . ?"

"While we go to our marriage class at church?" Dad finished.

Lucy nodded. Wasn't he the least bit uncomfortable about that class?

"Yes, you'll go to Claudette's this week. Then they'll be gone for two weeks."

Mom smiled at Lucy's dad. "Since Lucy did a lot of laundry today, I'll clean up the dishes myself." For two people fixing a marriage, they sure did smile at each other a lot.

"Then I'm going to my room," Lucy said. "Okay?"

She headed up the steps two at a time and closed her door firmly behind her. Once there, she went directly to her closet and opened the drawer that had the hidden compartment behind it.

At one time that secret compartment had held the letter that led to the hidden diary. Now it held another letter. The chain letter.

Urgent! she read again, scanning a bit. *If you do, you will have good luck for five days. . . . Jason in Louisiana won a cruise. . . . Missy in Illinois found a $100 check addressed to her in her mailbox. . . .*

Lucy drew a breath. *If you don't send this letter to five people within two days,* you *will be responsible for breaking the chain that all the other people have worked to build. Because of that, there will be consequences.* Bad *luck will come your way for five days, with the* worst *happening on the last day. . . .*

Lucy crossed her legs and sat down on the floor. Katie was her cousin—they'd loved each other their whole lives. Katie wouldn't send her something that wasn't good. In fact, Katie hated to send regular mail because it took so much time. So she must have felt this was really a good deal. She'd even had to go and copy the letter off.

And if Lucy got a cruise like Jason in Louisiana or one hundred dollars like Missy in Illinois, she could give someone a really *great* gift this week as her Diary Deed. Or maybe a cruise was just what Mom and Dad needed as a second honeymoon after putting their marriage back together! Lucy wouldn't tell them about the letter. This way, the cruise would be a great surprise.

And then there was that part about avoiding five days of bad luck.

She decided to do it.

Taking the letter with her, Lucy tiptoed downstairs into the little corner where her dad kept his home office stuff. Mom was still cleaning up in the kitchen, and Dad was upstairs reading.

A little corner of Lucy's mind stuck on what would happen to her friends if they didn't pass the letter on.

Maybe I'll be responsible for their bad luck.

Lucy turned the copier/printer on and waited for it to warm up. While she did, she decided to log on to her email account. She wasn't allowed on the Internet without an adult in the room, but she could write and answer email. Katie had scrawled at the bottom of the letter, *Email me and let me know you got this, okay?*

The cartoon screensaver disappeared as Lucy logged on. She had an email from Grammy, which she could answer later. She typed in Katie's address.

Hey! Lucy here. She pecked the letters out one by one. *I got the chain letter. I am copying it off right now. Email me back right away and tell me what great things happened to you! Love, your cous, Lucy.*

By the time Lucy had sent the mail, the copier was warmed up. She fed the chain letter through and pushed 5 for the number of copies she needed. The machine buzzed quietly as it spit out the letters. Lucy grabbed each one as it was expelled until she had a neat little stack. Then she walked upstairs again, quietly bypassing the kitchen and her parents' room. Just as she closed her door, she heard the telephone ring in the background.

"Now, for a little Jelly Belly snack," she said, pleased that good things would be rolling in this week. Lucy unsnapped the plastic Jelly Belly case that was next to her bedside and chose a Cream Soda bean and a Peach bean and chewed them together.

Mmm. Peaches 'n Cream.

Lucy took out the pad of paper and pencil she kept under her bed for important bursts of creativity and wrote out the names of five people she could send the letter to.

Serena, of course, was at the top of the list. She might win one hundred dollars, too!

Lucy scratched down Jenny's name and a couple of other girls on the Island.

"Lucy?" Mom's voice was just outside the door. "Can I come in?"

Lucy scooted the letters and her list back under her bed. "Sure, Mom."

"I have great news." Mom rushed in and sat beside Lucy on the bed. "I wanted to keep it a surprise until I knew all of the details, but you and I and Serena and her mother are going on a little overnight trip together. Mrs. Romero just called and said they could come!"

"We are?" Lucy jumped up. "When?"

"Tomorrow!"

Lucy threw her arms around her mother. What could

be more fun than a trip with her faithful friend? "Awesome."

Mom smiled. "We're going to stay on the *Queen Mary*, which is a luxury ship from way back. Now it's permanently anchored in Long Beach. We can take the ferry over, have fun together in the afternoon, just moms and daughters, and then all meet again for dinner. What do you say?"

"I say, okay! Can I call Serena and talk about it?"

"Of course. But quickly. You need to be off the phone by your nine o'clock curfew. We'll leave right after church tomorrow. Good thing you did the laundry," she added. "We'll have clean clothes to bring." Mom ruffled Lucy's hair. "You're becoming such a help to me, I can't tell you."

Lucy glowed. "Thanks for the trip idea, Mom."

Mom stopped before leaving the room. "I have a special reason for wanting to stay on the *Queen Mary*."

Lucy saw a mist of tears in her mother's eyes. "Are you okay?"

"Yes." Mom brushed her hand across her eyes. "I'll tell you all about it tomorrow."

Concern shadowed Lucy's heart till she saw her mother's smile return.

"Better make your call if you're going to," Mom finished.

No sooner had her mother left than Lucy dialed the phone. Serena answered.

"Hey, go to your window so we can see each other while we talk!" Lucy said.

"Great idea."

Lucy moved in front of her window and stared at

Serena's house, kitty-corner across their backyards. Serena had parted the little curtain in front of her triangle-shaped window.

"Did your mom tell you?" Lucy asked.

"Yes! I'm excited!"

"Me too. I'm packing right now. I can't believe we get to take a vacation together."

"Me neither. I'm trying to pack, too. Don't forget your sunglasses, and also something cool to wear to dinner. Maybe your new dress. I'll do your hair," Serena offered.

"Okay."

They hung up, and Lucy went back to packing. Tomorrow was Sunday, so that meant the second day after getting the chain letter would be Monday. Lucy would have to mail the letters from over town, in Long Beach, in order to mail them on time.

She quietly walked downstairs and got the Catalina phone book and five plain white envelopes. Before she went upstairs, Lucy checked her email—nothing from Katie . . . yet.

Then Lucy walked back to her room and tucked the phone book, chain letters, and envelopes into her backpack.

The Mysterious Brown Sack

Sunday . . . D Day minus five

The next morning Lucy awoke when her alarm went off at 8:03. She rolled out of bed after punching the snooze button a couple of times, and after breakfast she quickly dressed. On the walk to church, she sprayed some of her new breath freshener into her mouth. Mountain-fresh mint—guaranteed to smell sweet for up to forty-five minutes.

You never knew who might be at church.

Sure enough, Jake and his dad were the ushers. Lucy jockeyed to make sure she was on the side of the door where Jake was handing out bulletins.

"Good morning, Dr Pepper," Jake said. His brown hair was gelled back for the occasion. It looked nicer than usual.

"Good morning, Chief," Lucy teased back, the words

coming out in a puff of mint as she held back a giggle. Last week she had heard Jake's dad call him Chief and decided to call him that whenever he teased her about the Dr Pepper she preferred.

"It's a good day." He glanced at the bright island sun.

Lucy agreed. "And I'm glad I'm here." A moment later, as she joined her parents in a pew near the middle of the sanctuary, Lucy wondered if she'd meant she was glad to be on Catalina this summer, or at church again after years away. Or both.

Lucy waved to her friend Erica. *Won't she be glad to get one of the chain letters?* Claudette was also there with her parents, in the back.

The very last song they sang was one of Lucy's favorites. She had only been back to church for a couple of weeks, but she already loved the song that urged God to search her heart.

"Search my heart, Lord," she said softly at the conclusion. Then she sat down and fanned herself with the bulletin while the pastor began to speak. Lucy had begun to pay more attention to the pastor when she learned he was the father of Rachel, one of the teenagers who had been so kind to Lucy.

After the pastor taught and they had all prayed, the pastor called their attention once again. "If I may, can I see a show of hands from the people here who stuck their bulletins in their Bibles just now?"

Almost everyone raised a hand.

"Now," the pastor continued, "I don't want you to raise your hands this time, but I wonder how many of you still have the bulletin in your Bible from last week. Or how many of you just took it out this morning, not having opened your Bible since the end of last week's service. Just something to think about as you enjoy the blessing of this beautiful island and all that God has provided." He dismissed them, and Lucy and her family stood to go.

Not me, Lucy thought as they walked back to their cottage. *I'm not going to let my Bible sit there. Not after I learned last week how much God talks to me through it. I'll probably read it every day.*

Once they were home, Lucy's dad opened the squeaky screen and unlocked the door. "Get your stuff, and I'll drive you two down to the *Catalina Express,*" he said.

Lucy dashed upstairs. She had worn her capris and a nice shirt to church so she wouldn't have to change. She swapped shoes, grabbed her already-packed backpack, and was downstairs again before her dad had finished a glass of water.

"Mom? Ready?"

"Yes." Dad picked up the bags and headed outside to load them into the golf cart. "I guess you'll both do fine without me," he said.

Lucy knew he was teasing, but she saw sadness behind his eyes, too. "You can sleep with Tender Teddy tonight if you get lonely," she offered.

"Thanks. Are you sure you don't need a chaperone?"

"I'm sure, Dad," she said, kissing his cheek. He kissed her cheek in return.

A few minutes later they met Serena and her mother, who were already at the dock waiting.

They strolled up the small ramp to the ferry and took a seat inside. Lucy and Serena sat a few rows away from their moms so they could talk by themselves.

"Boy, am I glad to be going on this," Serena said as the ferry eased away from the dock.

"Me too. So much fun together," Lucy said.

"Well, that and other things."

"What's up?"

"It's Roberto's abuela. This morning she got really mad because she wanted to cook something and we didn't have any *hojas de aguacate*—avocado leaves. She uses them in a special sauce and basically said no self-respecting Mexican kitchen would be without them."

"Oh," Lucy said.

"So then," Serena said, "I told her that she had been kind of mean and bossy since she was here. So then my mom got mad at me and took me into the living room and told me I needed to learn to hold my tongue."

"I'm sorry," Lucy said. "I've said a lot of things I wish I hadn't."

"Yeah, well, I think if I need a lesson in holding my tongue, Abuela had better sit in on it." Serena's face grew deep pink. "I'm sorry. I guess I still haven't learned."

"It's okay." Lucy patted her friend's hand. "I know it's been stressful having her there."

As the ferry skipped along the gray blue water like a flat stone tossed from Catalina to Long Beach, the girls chatted the time away.

"So tell me about your urgent letter," Serena said.

"Well, it's a chain letter. From my cousin Katie—

remember I told you about her?"

Serena nodded.

"Anyway, if you send it to five people within two days of getting the letter, you will have fabulous luck for five days—like winning money or something. Isn't that fantastic?"

"What if you don't pass it on?"

"Well," Lucy squirmed a bit on the lemon-colored leather seat. "Then you'll have bad luck for five days, with the worst luck on the last day."

"Hmm," Serena said. "I think I'm glad I didn't get a letter like that."

Lucy glanced down at her backpack, which held the letter and yellow sticky paper with names written on it. "I have to go to the bathroom. I'll be right back."

As she stood up, Lucy took the backpack with her.

"Are you taking that thing? I can watch it," Serena said.

Lucy shook her head. Once in the bathroom, she took out the sticky paper and crossed Serena's name off the top. Now she was down to four names. She'd have to think of someone else to add.

She carried the pack back to their seats. In just a few minutes the ship pulled into port near the huge *Queen Mary*.

"Is that a boat or a floating city?" Lucy breathed out.

"Cool, eh?" Serena said. "I've seen it before, but I've never been on it—and I've lived nearby my whole life!" She smiled. "I'm glad we can share this together."

"Me too!" Lucy smiled back and looped her arm

through Serena's while they waited for their moms to come from their seats.

Lucy looked over the huge hull, its gray black body capped with white and deep sun orange. Portholes dotted the outside of the ship, like hundreds of perfectly round eyeglasses staring blankly at the boardwalk and water. When the moms got their bags together, the four of them left the ferry. Serena snatched a bit of wild jasmine and stuck it into her hair as they walked down the boardwalk and across the gangplank into the ship's lobby.

The lobby was draped in rich velvet. Lucy thought the place seemed more like a small town than a large hotel inside a ship that had carried three million passengers over its many trips.

"Did you see how many passengers the *Queen Mary* has carried?" Lucy whispered to her mother.

"Yes, and I know one of them. Someone important to me—and to you," her mom whispered back.

Just as Lucy was about to ask who in the world they knew who had been on this ship when it actually sailed, it was her mother's turn to check in. While Lucy waited, she read an information card that mentioned that the *Queen Mary*, from top to bottom, was taller than Niagara Falls.

After checking in and finding their way to their cabin, Lucy and Serena opened the door, raced into the room, and bounced on the beds. The springs sagged a bit and squeaked.

"Whee! Yipee!"

"Be careful! You'll break the beds!" Both moms giggled at them. Their room was comfortable, yet not large. It held two neatly made double beds, a table between them, and a small desk. The girls unpacked very little, and Lucy set her backpack so the letter faced down.

"How about you girls sleep toward the center and we moms on the outsides of the bed," Lucy's mom suggested. "That way we can get some beauty rest if you chatterers want to whisper all night."

The girls agreed, and Lucy and Serena set up a few things on the center table.

They put their things in the bathroom—Lucy and her mom's stuff on one side, Serena and her mom's stuff on the other. Then Serena's mom spoke up. "Shall we shop and explore a bit?"

"Together?" Serena asked. "All four of us?"

"Just you and me," Mrs. Romero said. "We can have some mother-daughter time."

"And then all meet back here before dinner," Lucy's mom said. She turned toward Lucy. "Visit the rest room, and then let's go!"

After Serena and her mom took off, Lucy said, "Well, what shall we do?"

"Tour the ship, of course!"

Lucy said nothing. She looked out her porthole and remembered the miles of hallways, dozens of exhibits, and hidden corners the boat's information card had promised.

"Wanna explore?" Lucy asked.

Mom got a funny smile. "You know, I do. I'll visit the rest room next. You grab some money out of my purse, and we'll go."

Lucy nodded and headed toward the little table where her mother had set her purse.

Once she opened it, Lucy located the money. Normally, her mother's purse held only a few items—brush, wallet, lipstick. This time Lucy spied a small brown leather sack, too. It seemed kind of heavy. Two cords pulled it tightly closed.

"Ready to go?" her mother asked.

"Yeah." Lucy handed her mom the money. "What's in this brown bag?"

Mom looked mischievous. "For that, my dear daughter, you will have to wait till tonight."

Disappeared!

Sunday evening . . .

First Lucy and her mom hit the exhibits. They wandered through the deck that had shops and cafés, browsing the old-time merchandise. Lucy bought a postcard from the old days and tucked it into her canvas bag—only three dollars. Next they went into a bookstore that sold magazines from every year from the past century.

"Maybe I can buy this one from 1932," Lucy said, thumbing through it. "You know, the old diary year."

Her mother pointed out the price. Forty-five dollars! Lucy handed it back to the cashier.

Next they went up to another deck with staterooms and mannequins dressed exactly as the real passengers fifty or so years ago would have dressed. They wore frilly dresses and wide hats. A restaurant—serving prune compote—was set up just as it would have been when the ship was packed with people traveling from England to New York. At one point, next to a war brides display, Lucy's mother pulled Lucy onto a polished bench nearby.

Why were they sitting down now? They'd just gotten started. . . .

"There is a special reason I wanted to come on this ship with you," Mom said. "I know you never knew *my* mother, your grandmother Anne. But she was a war bride. And she sailed on this ship."

Lucy stopped fidgeting. Her mom had never wanted to talk about her *own* mother before. They'd talked about her a little—Lucy knew she'd been from England. She knew her mom hadn't known her own mother very well before she'd died. Besides that, though, whenever Lucy had brought it up, her mom had said that it was in the past and they should always look forward.

"What's a war bride?" Lucy asked.

"When my dad was in World War II and stationed in England, he fell in love with my mom, who was a seventeen-year-old girl living in a nearby town. They got married, and after the war, she came over on the *Queen Mary* to live in America. She was a war bride."

Lucy sighed. "How romantic. They fell in love."

"Yes. The *Queen Mary* took in all kinds of war brides"—Mom pointed toward the models—"and brought them to their new families. Most of them never returned to their homeland. Your grandma was one of them."

"How come you never told me all of this before?"

Mom looked at her hands for a minute. "My mother died when I was young. She and my father had tried to have a baby for a long time, and by the time she had me,

33

they were older. When I was eight, she died of breast cancer. My dad didn't know what to do without her."

"I'm sorry." Lucy's heart leaked love and sorrow.

"I didn't know much what to do, either. I just sketched and painted and tried to stay out of my dad's way. He never wanted to talk about my mom or do girl things. So I didn't."

So that's why you've never painted your nails, Lucy thought, *or done other girly things with me.*

"I didn't know what it was like to have a mom, and my dad died not long after I went to college. I guess . . . I guess that's why, when I had you, I didn't know what to do as a mother. Sometimes things that seem so natural for other mothers aren't for me. Or I just do the wrong things. But I mean well. I try hard. I really do."

Lucy put her arm around her mother. "I love you. But why did you decide to tell me this now?"

Mom hugged Lucy. "When you and Serena started reading the diary, it brought back all this to me, since my mom kind of lived during that age, too, though she was a bit younger. We'll look in the attic when we get back to Seattle. I think I still have her old diary and letters."

Letters. It reminded Lucy of the chain letter. *I wonder what Mom thinks about luck.* Lucy decided to test her. "I guess it's good luck that we're here this summer," Lucy spoke up. "So you could show me all this."

"Good luck?" Mom shook her head. "Not luck. I think our coming to Catalina Island this summer is a reward. We're obeying God now, though we hadn't for a long time.

God is the Rewarder. I'm learning that He rewards us when we do the right thing."

Mom took Lucy's hand and pulled her up from the bench. "Now, let's finish the exhibits and shopping. Then to dinner"—she winked—"and my brown-bag surprise!"

☂ ☂ ☂

A couple of hours later, Lucy sat on the bed while Serena braided her hair.

"It's not as if the mayor herself will be there," Mrs. Romero teased them.

Lucy stood up and looked into the mirror. "It looks great. Could you please come over and do my hair every day?"

Serena giggled. "No. Get dressed, you goof. Ay yi yi." She rolled her eyes.

As they finished getting ready to leave, Lucy noticed her mother slipping the little brown bag into her fancy purse.

A few minutes later a *maître d'* escorted them into the elegant dining room. They sat near the window and looked out over the water. A waiter brought them some crystal glasses with cold water and a triangle lime slice in each.

"What do you want to drink besides water?" Lucy's mother asked the girls.

Serena whispered, "I think I want a Shirley Temple."

Lucy nodded her agreement and encouraged her friend to speak up. When the waiter reappeared, Serena said, "We'd like two Shirley Temples, please."

Serena smiled. Lucy grinned back. When the waiter returned, they each fished out a maraschino cherry and ate it first.

"Mama mia, fancy food on the menu!" Lucy said.

When it came time to order their dinner, Serena chose the sophisticated *rigatoni primavera*. Lucy chose whole roasted pheasant.

After a bit the waiter arrived with their meals. "And now, *mademoiselle*, whole roasted pheasant."

Even Lucy had to giggle. A small, whole animal—cooked, but looking somewhat like a mini chicken—was set before her. It didn't look like meat; it looked like the real thing. Tanned, with a neck where a head used to be. Maybe she'd just pick at the meat on the sides.

The lights grew dim, and twilight settled in for the evening. The waiter lit the tall candle in the center of their table. Lucy's mother motioned to the waiter to bend down, and she whispered something into his ear. In a minute he brought two small candles to the table.

What was this? Serena raised her eyebrows at Lucy, who shook her head as if to say, "I don't know!"

"I explained to Linda why I wanted her and Serena to come along this weekend." Lucy's mom smiled at Serena's mom. "One is, of course, because we are so pleased by and thankful for what wonderful friends you've been to us this summer." She stopped. "Of course, if I'd known what a good baker Linda was, I'd have been over there for bread sooner!"

Mrs. Romero laughed.

Lucy's mom went on to explain to Mrs. Romero and

Serena about Grandma Anne and the war brides. "Your sharing your grandmother's diary with Lucy, reading about your family history, made me feel like perhaps it was time to talk about my family and Lucy's. I wanted to share with you two as you have with Lucy. I'm realizing I let the sadness of my childhood color my life. I need to let go of the bad and pass on the good."

Lucy's mother took the small candle from in front of Lucy and lit it from the larger candle. "I'm going to pass on the good things from me to you," she said. Lucy's little candle flame danced merrily. "All the blessings I've been given."

After she was done, Lucy's mom nodded to Serena's mom. Serena's mother spoke quietly to her, too, and then lit the small candle in front of Serena.

"I have a little something for you," Serena's mother said. She took out a small envelope. Inside was a picture of Mrs. Romero's mother and grandmother.

"Ooh," Serena said. "This is the Serena who wrote the diary, right? With Grandma Peggy!"

"Right," her mom answered.

Serena stared at the picture and passed it to Lucy. Lucy looked it over. So cool—and so weird—to be looking at the face of the person whose diary she read each week. The old Serena looked like Lucy's friend Serena, too. She passed the picture back.

"I have something, too." Lucy's mom took the little brown sack out of her purse. "This was a ring my mom planned to give to me. It was the only thing she had saved from England. The stone is called an opal. One of her uncles had mined it himself in Australia. My dad did remember to give it to me when I was a teenager. And now I want to give it to you."

She slipped it over Lucy's middle finger. It was a bit big, but when Lucy held her fingers together tightly, it stayed on. When Lucy turned her hand, it caught the fire from the candles, and little crystal rainbows sparkled in the stone.

"Thanks, Mom. I'll treasure it always." Tears misted her eyes.

After dinner the girls went back to the room. When they were safely inside, the moms went out to get a cup of coffee from the café to bring back to the room.

Lucy sat down next to her backpack, getting ready to pull out her pajamas. But then she saw her other stuff. Instead of putting on her pj's, she opened up the chain letter.

She stared at it, saying nothing. Mom didn't believe in luck. Had Mom always believed that? Or was she just so thankful to be on the *Queen Mary* today because of Grandma Anne? The letter, which said it had been proven by hundreds of people, warned of bad luck if Lucy didn't act now. Suddenly, Lucy didn't know what to believe.

After a minute Serena came over and pointed at the letter. "Whatcha going to do with that?"

"Well . . . I guess I won't send them." Even as she said the words, Lucy heard her heart pound. *Five days! Bad luck!* Every other beat repeated in her head. *With the worst luck on the last day.*

"Why not?"

"Well, you didn't want me to send one to you, did you?"

Serena shook her head.

"I don't want to make other people scared about what could happen to them."

"Brave." Serena sat down beside Lucy. "It will probably work out all right."

Lucy nodded but didn't answer. She swallowed her gum, and it caught on its way down.

"Are you afraid of the bad luck?"

"I'm not sure." Lucy looked into her friend's eyes. *Might as well be honest.* "I'm a little nervous because I just don't know. A lot of people believe in luck. Most grown-ups even do."

Serena nodded but said nothing.

Throwing the letter away also meant there would be no cruise or money for a giant gift for Mom and Dad.

Once decided, Lucy acted quickly. She took all the copies of the chain letter and crumpled them into balls. Then she went into the bathroom and bombed them into the waiting can. The sticky note with names floated down last.

I'm doing the right thing, so God will reward me, not good luck. I don't have to worry about bad luck, she comforted herself. If only she knew that her mother was right.

"I'm going to wash my hands of the whole deal," Lucy said aloud, forcing her voice to sound braver than she felt.

She turned on the water to do just that and lathered her hands with lavender soap. As she stuck them under the sink to rinse them off, the precious opal ring that her mother had just given her slipped off and disappeared down the drain.

Lucy watched it slip away and turned the water off as fast as she could. *Oh no!* Had the bad luck already started?

"Serena! Help!" she cried.

First Deed Done Together

Sunday night, Monday morning . . .

"What is it?" Serena ran into the bathroom after Lucy called out to her.

Lucy pointed down the sink. "My new ring fell down there. Man alive. What will I do?"

Serena's eyes opened in shock. "We'll think of something. Can we reach a hanger in to get it?"

Lucy, the idea queen, went numb. "Okay." She raced into the main room and opened the closet. All of the hangers were the fancy thick ones, not the thin wire ones Lucy had in her closet at home. There was no way to bend one of those and try to reach the ring—if it was even there.

Lucy sat on the floor of the bathroom. The water was off. Her mom was sure to be back soon. Had the bad luck already started?

Just then they heard the door open.

"Come on." Serena took her hand. "I'll go with you."

When the girls walked back into the room, they were surprised to see not their mothers, but the housekeeper.

"Buenas noches," she said.

"Buenas noches," Serena replied. *"Como esta?"*

Lucy nodded politely, trying hard not to be sick on the carpet.

The housekeeper said something else in Spanish. Serena answered her.

"She came to turn down the beds for the evening," Serena said.

Just then Lucy spied the housekeeper's cart, filled with tools and supplies, in the hallway. "Do you think she has something that could help us?"

"Maybe!" Serena spoke briefly with the woman, who stepped out into the hall and brought back a long, thin wire with a hooked end.

The two girls followed her into the bathroom, where the housekeeper proceeded to stick the long wire into the sink's mouth and down its throat. After fumbling and muttering for a few minutes, she jiggled the wire and withdrew the ring.

She set it into Lucy's waiting hand. Lucy clasped her hand around the ring.

How could she show her thanks? *"Gracias,"* she said softly, feeling silly about using one of the few Spanish words she remembered.

"De nada," the woman said, waving her hand. She pointed to the curved neck pipes under the sink, showing

them where the ring had lodged—and remained safe.

After placing a mint on each pillow, the housekeeper left the room.

Lucy slipped the ring on her finger and squeezed her fingers tightly together. It couldn't be bad luck, because the ring was back.

"Whew." Lucy wiped a damp film of sweat off her forehead. "Well, now that the horror is over, let's do something fun," she said to Serena. "I brought a 'future quiz.' We can both fill it out. You pick what kind of job you want when you grow up, what you want your husband to look like, your house, stuff like that."

"Fun!" Serena sat down cross-legged on the bed while Lucy dug through her stuff for the quiz. "Are you going to tell your mom about losing the ring?"

Lucy stopped what she was doing. "I guess so . . . eventually. I just want to let the stress pass for a while first."

The girls filled out their papers, Lucy writing in Serena's answers and Serena writing down Lucy's answers.

"We can put this in our diary," Serena suggested.

"Great idea. Hey, I noticed that your future husband seems to look a lot like Philip."

"Ha! Not really," Serena said. "And I suppose your future job will be owning an ice-cream shop?" Jake's family owned the town's ice-cream and candy store.

"No way." Lucy giggled. They both drew pictures of what they wanted their houses to look like.

"How many kids do you want?" Serena asked. "I think I want three."

"I don't know," Lucy said, thinking of herself, the only

child, and Claudette, with her new sister. "Anything more than just one."

Serena said nothing, and a few minutes later the mothers returned.

"You girls okay?" Lucy's mom asked.

Lucy looked at Serena. "Yes," she said. Then she silently mouthed, "Tomorrow morning," to Serena. She'd tell Mom in the morning after they'd relaxed for a while. That way it wouldn't spoil this special night.

🌂 🌂 🌂

The next morning came soon, after the girls had spent until three in the morning whispering together. Lucy woke up feeling like someone had hit her over the head. She didn't feel like getting out of bed.

"How about breakfast in bed before we check out?" Mom offered.

"Ah, Mom, the perfect idea. No whole roasted pheasant today." Lucy opted for scrambled eggs and chocolate chip pancakes. Serena wanted waffles with strawberries and whipped cream.

When the room-service man rolled the cart into the room, it reminded Lucy of the housekeeper the night before. She needed to tell her mother.

The girls cleaned their plates, and while Serena and her mom were in the bathroom brushing their teeth, Lucy spoke up.

"Mom? Can I talk with you for a minute?"

"Sure." Mom stepped over and sat in the chair across the table from Lucy.

"Well, I had a little accident last night."

Her mom's eyes narrowed. "What happened?"

"I was washing my hands, and the new ring fell off, down the sink."

Mrs. Larson's eyes flew open and then immediately glanced at Lucy's middle finger. She breathed out when she saw the opal ring there in the middle, right next to the Navajo turquoise one on the fourth finger. "I see you found it."

"Yes. The housekeeper came in to turn down the beds. She helped us get it out."

"Would you like to keep it in the brown sack till we get home so you don't have to worry about it?"

Lucy sat still. She could see that was what her mom wanted to happen. "I guess." She reluctantly took off the ring and slipped it into the brown sack, which she set inside her backpack.

"Thanks for telling me, Luce. You're growing up. It was good to share those happy and sad things with you yesterday."

Lucy nodded.

Mom nodded, too. "I've been thinking. I'd like to do some of those girlish things I missed growing up. I'm going to make a special lunch for you this week. I'll make it myself, and we'll eat it together. Ladies only."

Lucy nodded and stood up to finish packing. "Okay."

As her mother went to check out of the hotel, Lucy

zipped up her backpack. The Catalina phone book was still there, but no letters.

"Was your mom mad about the ring?" Serena asked.

"No, I guess not. Thanks to that wonderful house-keeper."

"Yeah. I'm so glad she was here."

Lucy faced Serena. "I'd like to do something for her."

"We could pray for her," Serena suggested.

"Okay." Lucy and Serena bowed their heads together and each took a turn praying for the woman—for her happiness, that she wouldn't have to work too hard, and for her to know Jesus better, whether she knew Him already or not.

As soon as they finished praying, Lucy jumped up from the chair. "I have it!"

Serena looked at her, puzzled.

"Instead of doing *one* Diary Deed, let's each give a secret gift to someone every day till Diary Day. We can pray for that person and write a secret note. We can ask them to pass good things on, like my mom said last night. But only if they want to. It's like the best parts of the chain letter, without the bad."

"Okay!" Serena agreed.

"See? Throwing the chain letter away was the right thing to do. And getting the ring back to wear forever was a reward for doing the right thing." Lucy hummed as she searched for some paper to write the note on.

But I don't have the ring now, do I? Lucy rubbed the finger that felt cool and lonely since the opal had been put into the brown bag.

She brushed away bad thoughts. *I'll get it back at home. For good.*

Lucy whipped out a piece of the complimentary stationery from the desk drawer and handed it to her friend. Serena wrote a note in Spanish to the housekeeper, telling her how thankful they were that she was there to help, what a blessing she'd been, and that they had prayed for her.

Serena folded the note and wrote *Doña Sirviente* on it. They left it on the table, where she'd be sure to find it.

"Don't forget this!" Lucy said, choosing the freshest jasmine of the wild few Serena had picked at the ferry terminal yesterday.

Serena took the jasmine blossom from Lucy's hand and placed it on top of the letter.

"Okay," Lucy said. "We did the first present together. But the rest of them have to be secret, okay? No fair telling each other until Friday."

They went into the bathroom to pack up their gear. Serena pointed to the garbage can, stuffed with the wadded-up chain letters. "Worried about the bad luck anymore?"

"Kind of. But my decision is made."

Serena nodded. "There are four days after today of secret gift-giving till D Day. And four days after today of the supposed bad luck that letter threatened," she said.

"Including the final day." Lucy set her jaw. "By the end of this week, we'll know—will good deeds or bad luck win out?"

Lucy's mother came back to collect the girls, and she

put a tip for the housekeeper on the table. When everyone else was heading toward the door, Lucy slipped two dollars of her baby-sitting money out of her wallet and placed it with the letter.

Serena wrote the note, and I left the money. Together!

It wasn't until they boarded the ferry that Lucy realized the housekeeper would believe only Spanish-speaking Serena had left both the note and the money, since they had been put in the envelope together.

It shouldn't really bother me. But Lucy had wanted the lady to know how thankful *she* was, and now she never would.

She stared at the water, watching the waves clip by, her stomach swimming inside of her. What would this week hold? Tomorrow, even?

Gone for Good

Monday evening . . . D Day minus four

Lucy's dad met them at the ferry terminal with Serena's dad, who was still on vacation. Lucy and Serena smiled at each other, watching their dads chat like old fishing buddies.

"I'll meet you at the beach tomorrow morning, okay?" Serena said as she stepped into her golf cart.

Almost no one on Catalina drove cars. Instead, they zipped around in golf carts. Lucy was hoping to decorate theirs with groovy bumper stickers just for fun. She hadn't asked her dad yet. Someone on the Island had a cart decorated like a Mercedes Benz, and another one looked like a horse! It was so much more fun than plain golf.

"See you at the beach!" Lucy promised, knowing some of the other girls would be there, too. Since Jenny had admired her turquoise ring, Lucy couldn't wait to show her the new opal ring.

They drove toward home, stopping by the post office first. When they pulled up in front and her dad cut the motor, Lucy's stomach lurched.

"Can you run in and get the mail, Sparky?" Dad asked.

Lucy breathed deeply. "I guess so." *Hope there aren't any more "urgent" letters.*

She stepped out of the cart and took the keys from her dad's hand. She stepped into the post office and slipped the key into the lock. Two magazines, that was all.

Lucy smiled and her shoulders relaxed.

They arrived at home, and while her dad opened the door, Lucy noticed the jasmine blossoms finally flowering on the front vine. She stuck her nose into the center of a flower, holding it there for a minute, hovering like a little bumblebee. *Sweet.* She plucked a couple of blossoms and brought them upstairs. She had no idea who she'd give her next Diary Deed to, but she'd be ready.

"I think I'll go take a rest," her mom announced. Dad had already carried the suitcases upstairs.

"Tired?" he asked Lucy as she came downstairs again.

"Nah," she answered.

"Want to play a game of chess? I worked a bit after church yesterday, so we could spend some time together this afternoon."

Lucy looked at her dad with happy surprise. "Okay." Work almost always took first place in his life, and always had. It was one of the reasons she had been worried about staying on Catalina with them this summer.

They pulled up the two lumpy chairs in the living room, which was really Mom's art studio. A blank canvas stood in the corner, white like a clean bed sheet. Mom would start something new soon. And then maybe she'd be lost in her work, too.

But for now, a good match of chess was in order. Lucy made the first move.

Her dad considered his response. "I see you noticed the blooming *Jasminum officinale*."

"What?" Lucy said.

"The vine at the front. You picked some blossoms."

"Oh, Dad. *Jasmine*."

"Just what I said," he answered. He made a move.

Lucy considered her response.

"I think it smells nice," she said, making her move. "Do you?"

"Um-hmm." Dad made his move. "Did you have a good time with your mom and Serena and Mrs. Romero?"

"The best. Serena is the best friend I ever had." Lucy moved her piece.

"Did you like the ship?" Dad asked, making another move.

"Yes . . ." She set her piece down and looked at her dad's face. "Did you know about Grandma Anne and the *Queen Mary*?"

"I did," he answered. "Though we hadn't talked about it much. I'm glad Mom talked with you about it."

"I'm growing up," Lucy answered, finally moving.

"You are." Her dad checkmated her. "But you can't match the old man in chess."

"Not this game, anyway," Lucy joked. *I wonder what Dad thinks about luck.* "You lucked out," she said.

"Not luck," he responded. "Lots of years of practice and playing. And an opponent whose mind isn't all there today for some reason."

Lucy *had* lost rather quickly. Sometimes their games went on for hours. This time, though, her mind was elsewhere. Lucy stood up and hugged her dad, his beard tickling her neck in the way it always had since she was a little girl.

"I hope this growing-up Lucy has time for her old dad," he said.

Lucy looked at him. She couldn't tell if he was serious or joking.

"Well," she said, hoisting out of the lumpy armchair and walking toward the stairway. "Don't worry, Dad. I'm not getting rid of Tender Teddy yet, either."

Her dad roared in laughter and set the chess game back up for a rematch later.

Once upstairs, Lucy noticed that her mom had unpacked some of her clothes. That was nice. Lucy took the little candle from last night's dinner and set it on her dresser. She wasn't allowed to light candles in her room, but it sure smelled good.

She set the notebook with the quizzes aside. *Gotta put those in our best friends' diary,* she thought, tidying up. She settled the Woodstock she and Serena had bought last week at Knott's Berry Farm on her bed next to Tender Teddy.

After everything was put away, she remembered something odd. *Where is the brown bag with the opal ring?* It had been in her backpack.

It wasn't anywhere.

Please, God, don't let it be lost again.

Her mouth dry, Lucy searched all over her room, in the compartments of the backpack, under the bed, on the desk and dresser. She looked under the covers, although how it could have ended up there she had no idea. Her head felt light again. Could it have fallen out? Finally she decided she had better go and ask her mother.

Lucy knocked lightly on her parents' bedroom door and opened it to find her mom resting on the bed, reading.

"Mom?"

"Yes?"

Lucy walked into the still room. "Thanks for helping me unpack. Did you . . . did you put my opal ring somewhere?"

"Oh yes," her mother said, sitting up. Part of her face was pink from lying on the pillow. "I took it."

Relief washed over Lucy like a splash of warm water.

"I meant to talk to you about that. I've been thinking. It might be better if I keep it for now. I should have known better. You're just not quite big enough. Silly me. I was sixteen or something when I got it, and here you are, just barely twelve, though a great twelve at that."

Lucy's heart dropped. Hadn't her mother just said she was growing up? Now she didn't trust her?

Mom must have seen the look on Lucy's face, because she said, "Oh, don't worry, honey. The ring will still be yours. It's not your fault at all. I'm just keeping it safe—for both of us."

Her mom lay down again. "I'm going to rest for a bit longer, and then we'll start dinner, okay?"

Lucy opened her mouth to say something but closed it up quickly before angry lava erupted from deep inside. Lucy was about to tell her mother just what she thought of this new decision, but she remembered Serena talking about learning to hold her tongue.

Lucy turned on her heel and practically ran back to her room.

The ring was gone for good. Well, it might just as well be for good. Till she was sixteen, anyway. It was her only link with Grandma Anne, a symbol of Lucy's new relationship with her mother.

Snatched away.

Once her door was slammed shut, Lucy grabbed her notebook and scribbled out angry words—words that told her mother she felt ripped off and that everything they had talked about was a mistake, and how come she didn't think about this sixteen thing before she even made such a big production and gave the ring to Lucy. Her mother was right yesterday, after all. Mom did do wrong things. Period.

Then Lucy remembered what her mother had softly said after that. *But I mean well. I try hard. I really do.*

Lucy sat on the floor and held the tears back, squeezing her eyes shut so tightly that she saw shadows and dots inside her eyelids. She breathed out and looked at the letter.

Instead of giving the letter to her mom, she rolled it up into a big ball and stared at it. She needed to think. She wasn't ready to throw it away, if she ever would be. Lucy tossed the wadded-up note under her bed, way back where the dust clouds floated—barely touching the wooden floor.

The balled-up letter reminded Lucy about the chain

letter she'd tossed away and all that it had promised, both good and bad.

Wearing the ring after it had been recovered from the sink was going to be a sign to her that there was no bad luck coming to get her. It was only the first day after throwing the letters away.

What does this mean?

Telephone

The next morning Lucy ran downstairs to see if there was an email from Katie. There wasn't. *Maybe Katie didn't send out enough letters and something bad happened.* Lucy typed up another quick one asking if Katie was still alive and then headed off to meet her friends.

Once at the beach, Jenny and Serena and Lucy formed a triangle and played Frisbee. Someone set up a volleyball net and they tried to play, but there were too many tourists on the beach. Then they swam for a good hour. Some of the kids went home afterward, and the others sat down. Some older sisters and their friends joined Lucy and Serena's usual crowd.

"Let's play Telephone," someone suggested. "It's something we can do while we're sitting."

Lucy thought that was a bit strange, since she hadn't played that game for a few years, but a rest would be good.

Lydia started by whispering in someone's ear. The next girl, someone's older sister, was next, and then it went round the group.

When it came to Lucy, she changed it from "Jenny is a good friend" to "Jenny is a really great friend."

Finally, the first round ended with the last person in the loop saying the phrase out loud.

After a few more good comments, Lucy began to notice that someone was turning things bad—saying mean things. When it came to "Erica has a big nose," Lucy changed it to "Erica has great clothes." Erica had been a good friend ever since she'd helped with the little lost dog a couple of weeks ago.

At the end, when it was said out loud, no one looked surprised by the change. Lucy didn't know who had started the big nose comment.

The sand was starting to scratch under Lucy's leg. For some reason the sun felt hotter than it had a few minutes earlier.

The next round of Telephone ended with Betsy biting her nails. It hadn't been that when Lucy had heard it! Betsy tried to giggle, but her face fell and her braids tumbled down as she looked at the beach.

Betsy was the second person on Catalina to have been nice to Lucy, and she was kind of new, too. Lucy wished she were close enough to squeeze Betsy's hand.

After a few more rounds, the phrase "Lucy is from up north" reached Lucy's ear. After it had passed on, the game ended with Jenny this time. She spoke softly.

"Lucy has a big mouth."

Lucy held her breath and said nothing, not wanting to look down but not wanting to look at anyone else, either. Her face felt as hot as the sun.

"You know what? No offense, but I hate this game," Erica said. "I'm going home for lunch."

The other girls scattered, and Lucy walked quickly toward town before anyone could talk to her.

More bad things happening to me. Bad plus bad equals bad. And this is only day two.

Serena was the only one who caught up. "Are you okay?"

"Yeah," Lucy said.

"They said something bad about almost everyone. Not just you. I don't know who started it. I bet it was one of the older girls who doesn't even know you."

"Yeah," Lucy said. "Probably true. But that's the problem with gossip. People can say mean things and pass it on, and no one has to own up to saying it."

Serena nodded. "Want to get a Dr Pepper?"

"If you don't mind, I'd like to be alone because I'm going to do my Diary Deed secret gift, okay?"

"Okay," Serena said. "Call me later."

Lucy nodded and managed a weak smile, dragging toward town still thinking about that lame Telephone game. She was glad she had changed the last thing about Serena that had come around—"Serena is a weak noodle." Lucy had changed it to "Serena draws a good doodle." Lucy wouldn't want anyone to feel like this.

Why did Jenny have to say, "Lucy has a big mouth," out

loud? Lucy's chest squeezed hard, and her breaths came faster. Not Jenny!

Lucy couldn't believe what was happening. This was the second day of the five.

She decided to get a Dr Pepper after all, and it cheered her up a little. After she polished off the cold pop, Lucy walked to the pharmacy and selected a bottle of inexpensive nail polish, determined to do something good in spite of what was going on. Lucy loved the polish color so much she bought some for herself, too.

Poor Betsy. The meanness had started with the comment about her bitten nails. Lucy wrote *Betsy* on the brown bag and, while walking toward Betsy's house, plucked a jasmine blossom off a bush that flowered over the sidewalk.

Lucy had purchased a little card, too, and wrote in it: *You are a sweet person with a sweet heart and pretty nails. If you like, pass a blessing on to someone else, but keep it a secret!* Then she prayed for Betsy.

She ran up to Betsy's front step, left the package there, and hurried away.

Once around the corner, where no one could see her, she giggled. It's not that the Telephone comment didn't hurt. It still stung. But doing this for Betsy felt really, really good and pushed that bad feeling a little farther back.

Hey! If Lucy painted her nails the exact same color, Betsy might guess that it was Lucy who had left it. And they'd become even better friends!

She'd paint her own nails when she got home. Serena had always done it for her, but Lucy could try, too, couldn't she?

Feeling better, she picked up the pace and let her flower-powers flip-flop her home. When she got there, her mother was humming in the kitchen, pouring the last bit of tea into her glass before washing the sun-tea jar.

"Hi," Lucy said.

"Hi there, honey," her mom answered, hugging her. Lucy felt the ice toward her mother crack a bit.

Lucy walked upstairs and tossed her wallet down. She sat down on the floor next to her bed and looked over her toenails. Should she paint them, too? As she stared at her toes, she caught a glimpse of the wadded-up paper still hiding under her bed.

She didn't pull it out and throw it away yet. But she didn't want to look at it right now, either.

Lucy grabbed the new polish, some cotton balls, and a bottle of remover. *Maybe Mom would like her nails painted, too.* When Mom had given Lucy some polish for her birthday a few weeks back, she had told Lucy she'd never painted her own nails.

"Mom?" she called, prancing down the steps.

Her mom was still in the kitchen with the half-full glass of sun tea. "I suppose you're hungry—right?"

"Not really." Lucy held up the bottles of polish. "I had an idea. Can I paint your nails? You said you've never done it, and I thought, well, maybe it's because you didn't really have a mom and didn't do those girlish things. You have a daughter, though, so maybe it would be fun to do it together."

Lucy held her breath. What would Mom say?

Her mom laughed. "Okay, honey. Kind of strange to

be a painter who has never had painted nails, eh?"

Lucy sat down next to her mom. "Spread your hands out, and I'll do your nails. Look at this cool new color!"

Lucy saw her mother's eyes fly open at the green. "Well, okay. If you say so."

Lucy shook the bottle of paint and delicately painted each one of her mother's nails. When they were dry, she painted on a second coat and then sprayed them with some polish dryer that Serena had loaned her.

Mom held her nails up. They were the color of Kermit the Frog with the stomach flu.

Lucy giggled a little, and soon they were both laughing out loud.

Just then Lucy's dad walked into the kitchen. "What's going on here?"

"Want your nails painted?" Lucy asked.

"Ah, no thanks," he said. "But I do feel a little left out, with all the girl stuff going on around here. Tonight is Mom's and my class at church, but how about if tomorrow night you and I take a scenic drive in the golf cart together?"

"Okay," Lucy agreed.

As Lucy sat down, her mother spoke up. "Since you did that for me, how about if I braid your hair before you go to Claudette's tonight? Like I used to when you were a little girl."

"That would be really nice," Lucy said. After lunch, she went in search of two pony twists so her mom could make English braids.

🐜 🐜 🐜

Later that evening Lucy's parents dropped Lucy off at Claudette's house while they went to their marriage class at church. Lucy smiled when Mom waved good-bye to her, green nails and all. It warmed her heart that Mom hadn't taken the polish off before the class with all the other adults.

Lucy found Claudette in her room, stuffing almost everything she owned into a slightly beat-up suitcase.

"Ooh, look at those braids." Claudette ran into the bathroom and then ran back into her room with a brush and two pony twists. "Can you braid my hair like that? We'll look like twins."

Twins. As in sisters. Claudette sat down on her chair, and Lucy stood behind her, brushing her hair out.

"Are you excited to get your sister?" Lucy asked.

"Yes. We're going to name her *Chantal Lian*. Lian means *graceful willow*. It's her Chinese name."

"Cool," Lucy said. "We'll still be kind of sisters, too, though. Right?"

Claudette turned around, loosening the braid Lucy was weaving. "Of course. But now I'll have a real sister, too." She looked down. "I'm really sorry that you can't, too."

Lucy sucked air. When Claudette stood up to go put the brush back into the bathroom, Lucy pulled from her canvas bag two pairs of socks she had purchased on the *Queen Mary*. She stared at them. She had meant to slip them into Claudette's suitcase. One pair was Claudette's size; one was a pair of baby socks.

But now that Claudette had to remind her about the fact that she, Lucy, would never have a sister, Lucy didn't feel like being so nice. She knew it wasn't Claudette's fault, but . . .

Claudette is getting everything important. It felt hard to give her something more.

Do the right thing. Lucy knew that she was giving to Claudette because she wanted to bring her joy, like the diary girls said, and not because of what Claudette would do or say in return. But it still hurt.

Lucy sighed and slipped the socks into the suitcase. Her heart ached when she let go of the tiny socks. *A baby sister.*

Claudette raced back into the room. "Wanna hear me play 'Chicken Sticks'?"

Lucy's eyes opened wide. " 'Chicken Sticks'?!"

"I mean 'Chap Sticks.' "

Lucy was still puzzled.

"I mean 'Chopsticks.' Do you want to hear me play 'Chopsticks' on the piano? You *are* my best piano teacher, you know," Claudette said.

"Personally," Lucy said, "I think 'Chicken Sticks' sounds more interesting. But yeah, I'll listen to you play 'Chopsticks.' "

She followed Claudette out to the living room. Claudette sat down to play, and Lucy glanced at the Chinese calendar hung above the piano. Tomorrow was Wednesday, the day Claudette and her parents left for China.

Day three, according to the chain letter.

Tuesday hadn't gone well at all. Surely *tomorrow* would

be the day when good things, rewards, would start coming to Lucy.

She didn't believe in bad luck. She didn't.

Did she?

8

Rachel to the Rescue

Wednesday . . . D Day minus two

Serena arrived at Lucy's house right at ten the next morning.

"Another day!" Serena announced. "Whatcha want to do?" she asked.

Another day. What would it hold? Lucy steeled her heart. Today would be good! She'd make it be.

"You know what we haven't done this week?" Lucy said. "We haven't visited the dogs."

Two weeks earlier Lucy and Serena had helped find a home for a stray dog about to have puppies. Lucy was getting one of the pups, but they had to stay with the mother dog for a few more weeks.

"Great! I'll call Mrs. Marshall and see if we can come over." Serena dialed the number of the woman from her church who was caring for the dogs right then.

"Hello, Mrs. Marshall? This is Serena. Lucy and I were wondering if we can come over and visit the puppies this morning."

Lucy couldn't hear what Mrs. Marshall said, but she could sure hear a loud voice on the other end.

She watched as Serena pursed her lips. "Okay. Thank you. Good-bye."

She clicked the phone off and handed it back to Lucy. "She said not today."

"What else did she say?" Lucy asked, walking over to the counter and hanging up the portable phone.

Serena just shook her head, her face still flushed. "I guess she's having a bad day. And I'm trying to learn to hold my tongue. Let's just make some other plans, okay?"

Lucy nodded. "How about pedal boating? We have popcorn in here somewhere."

Serena brightened. "Great idea."

Lucy took out a bag of microwave popcorn and popped it. She and Serena walked toward the Green Pleasure Pier, where they could rent a pedal boat for a short time.

"How are your Diary Deeds going?" Lucy asked.

"Fine—but don't try to get me to tell you anything," Serena teased. "Not till Friday, anyway."

A few minutes later they arrived at the Green Pleasure Pier. Lucy scanned the water. "A lot of the others are already out there boating."

"Yeah." Serena looked at Lucy. "Is that okay with you?"

"Yes." Lucy stared out at the choppy water. "I guess

they didn't mean anything bad yesterday. But let's try to go in our own area."

She and Serena put on their life vests and pedaled out to where the others were. Erica waved to them, calling, "Come on over!"

Lucy dropped a trail of popcorn behind them. "Hansel and Gretel meet the sea," she joked. The fish jumped up and gulped the popcorn as soon as she dropped it.

"Just like the birds in the fairy tale," Serena said.

They pedaled over to Betsy and her sister.

"Hi," Betsy said. "How are you two?"

"Good," Serena answered.

Lucy looked at Betsy's green fingernails and smiled. She flashed her own toward Betsy, hoping she'd notice they matched.

Betsy saw Lucy glance over at her nails. "Isn't this a wild color?" she whispered to Lucy. "Someone left it at my house yesterday. I think it was Julie. Don't tell her, but I'm going to give her a secret present back."

Lucy's heart sank. So much for the gift's drawing Betsy and Lucy closer together. This had not worked out as she had hoped.

The gift was about Betsy, Lucy reminded herself. *Not about me.*

Lucy could see Jenny paddling toward them. Her heart still felt icy toward Jenny from the Telephone game yesterday. She wished it didn't, but it did.

Lucy pedaled her part of the boat so that even though they were all very close and could talk with one another, she wouldn't have to meet Jenny's gaze. She just wasn't ready for that yet.

"So who's excited about camp next week?" Betsy asked.

"Of course we are!" everyone chimed in.

Lucy looked at Serena and whispered, "Is everyone going to camp next week?"

Serena nodded.

"Even you?"

Serena nodded again. "We go the same week every year. There are two Christian camps on the Island. We talked about it a little at your birthday party, but we've been so busy since then. . . ."

"Oh."

The water grew silent except for the greedy smackings of the fish.

"I wish you could come, too, Lucy," Betsy said.

"Yeah," almost everyone chimed in. But the water had grown quiet again.

Day three. More bad luck, I guess. Even though I thought I didn't believe in it.

"We'd better get the boat back," Betsy said. "Or we'll have to pay a fine."

After a few minutes only Lucy and Serena remained on the water, since they had rented their boat later.

"I'm sorry about camp. It's fun. Your friend Rachel is always one of the counselors on the week we're there. . . ."

Suddenly Serena snapped her fingers. "Let's ask Rachel if there are any openings! She'd be sure to know."

Lucy's head rose. "Serena, *you* might accidentally be a genius! I'll go right home and check with my parents."

They pedaled in as fast as they could. "Call me as soon as you know!" Serena said. Lucy ran as fast as she could to her house. When she got home, she barely had enough breath to choke out the idea to her mother.

"Hey! I thought we were going to spend time with the family this summer!" her mom said.

"We are, we *are*!" Lucy pleaded. "The camp's only one week. Not even."

Her mother relented. "All right. It's a Christian camp. Call Rachel and see if they have any spaces left."

Lucy dug out the phone book and dialed Rachel's number.

"May I speak to Rachel, please?"

"One moment."

Lucy hurriedly spread peanut butter on a piece of bread and chopped it into two squares while she waited. She tossed the knife into the sink.

"Hello?"

"Hi, it's Lucy."

"Oh, Lucy, I missed you at Power Hour this week."

Power Hour. With the trip and all, she'd forgotten.

Lucy explained why she was calling.

"I'll find out," Rachel said. "Come to church tonight and I'll let you know. You can help me rearrange the books in the library. I know you like to read. Maybe I'll have an answer for you by then."

Lucy quickly asked her mom, who agreed. "I'll see you then!" Lucy promised.

In a few hours, I'll know.

🌴 🌴 🌴

Right after dinner Lucy's dad drove her to the church. "I'll be back to pick you up in about an hour for our sunset drive together."

"Okay, Dad."

Lucy hopped out of the golf cart and walked up the stone pathway to the little white-and-green church. Jake's yellow flowers still bloomed in front.

"Hi!" Rachel waited for her right inside. "Have you ever been to the library?"

"Nope," Lucy said. She didn't want to rush Rachel, but she really wanted to know—were there any openings?

"Follow me, then." Rachel headed downstairs. Just off to the side was a tiny, cut-out library. Three cozy chairs huddled there—a large one, a medium-sized one, and a kid-sized one. Lucy wondered if the Three Bears had been by recently. The room smelled of paper—old and new.

"Can you help me file all these?" Rachel pointed to a couple of book boxes. "Oh, and the camp should be calling back soon, too."

Well, that answered that question.

On top was a book on Native American Christians. "Can I borrow this?" Lucy asked.

"Of course," Rachel said. "You belong to this church!"

The phone rang upstairs.

"I'll go get it. It's probably the camp."

Lucy sat still and prayed.

Jenny

Wednesday evening . . .

When Rachel returned to the library, she wasn't smiling. "I'm sorry, Lucy. The camp is full next week. They've been booked up for a long time."

Lucy's head bobbed down.

"Sometimes they have a last-minute opening," Rachel said. "I told them to call me right away if they do."

"Okay," Lucy said. "Thanks for trying." She shuffled a book on death into the open slot on the library shelf.

"Not a good day?" Rachel asked.

Lucy sighed. She might as well admit it, even to herself. "Not a good week."

"Want to talk about it?" Rachel asked.

The stuff with her mom and with Jenny stung the most right now. Besides camp, of course, and Rachel already knew about that. Lucy asked, "Rachel, what do *you* do if people say things that hurt you?"

"It all depends," she said. She put her book down and plunked down cross-legged next to Lucy. "If it's something that's going to make a difference to me, a big deal in a relationship, then I have to say something to that person."

"What about holding your tongue?" Lucy said.

"Well, I think that's different. Saying something in a big explosion of anger right on the spot isn't a good idea. It doesn't mean you can't say something later, when you've mellowed out."

Lucy nodded.

"It's no good holding your tongue if you're going to hold a grudge, too," Rachel said. "And it seems like whatever you're thinking about still bugs you a lot."

Lucy rubbed the finger where the opal ring used to sit. It still bugged her. A lot.

"So you always tell someone if you're angry, right? Even if you don't tell them right then?"

"Well, no. A lot of the times I get over being angry and it's not worth it. If it's something that was a mistake, or if it's not at all how that person normally treats me, then I figure I should just blow it off." She grinned. "I'll show you."

Rachel stood up and took a daisy out of the vase on the table between the three bears' chairs. She threw the other two dead daisies into the nearby trash can. She plucked all the petals into her open palm. Then she held it up to her mouth and said, "I forgive you." She blew hard, and the petals scattered everywhere.

Rachel laughed. "I normally just do this in my mind, though. Otherwise I'd be vacuuming all the time."

Lucy scooted around on the floor with Rachel, picking up the daisy petals. They had landed on the shelves and under the table, and one stuck to Lucy's knee as she crawled around. She peeled it off and then bonked her head on the table. She and Rachel both burst out in laughter.

"I can honestly say I never thought I'd be scouting petals tonight," Lucy giggled. When they finished the task, Lucy took her book and went upstairs to meet her dad.

He pulled up soon thereafter. "Hop in! I have a little store I want to get to."

Lucy jumped in, and the golf cart jerked away from the curb. Soon they pulled up at a small plant nursery.

"Uh, Dad, are you working tonight after all?"

"Nope. Come on."

They walked into the store, even though its outsides were as crammed with plants as the inside was. All sorts of living lovelies showed their flowering faces in a room that smelled like steamed grass clippings. Lucy's dad went right over to a shelf where the African violets were.

"I used to have one of these," Lucy said. "Before it gave up and died."

"I thought maybe we could buy you another one."

"I'm tired of being responsible for plant deaths," Lucy said. "Even though that purple frilly one is pretty."

"I'll help you," Dad said. "It's one thing you and I can do together."

Lucy looked at his face and remembered how lonely he had seemed when Lucy and her mother went to the *Queen Mary* without him . . . and his face when he saw them giggling together painting Mom's nails.

"Okay," she said. "If anyone can help me, you can."

Her reward was a big smile peeking out from behind a well-trimmed beard.

They went to the counter to pay for the violet, and Lucy spied some cut daisies.

"Can I buy a few of these?" she asked her dad. "They're cheap." He nodded.

She picked out the prettiest three of the bunch and wrapped a thin ribbon around the stalks. In her tiniest letters she printed on one of the complimentary gift cards: *To Rachel: If I had a sister, I'd want her to be like you. If you want, pass this blessing on.*

As they walked out to the golf cart, Lucy bent over and picked up a jasmine blossom that had dropped from one of the nearby bushes and tucked it in with the daisies.

"Can we stop by the church before our drive?" she asked. "For just a minute."

Lucy ran up the church steps and left the gift right inside the door, where she knew Rachel would have to pass before she went home. She turned to leave.

As she did, she saw a stack of bulletins on the windowsill, leftovers from Sunday's service.

Not only had she missed Power Hour, but Lucy had not opened her Bible once since Sunday.

She closed her eyes again. "I'm sorry, God. I've been so caught up in my problems that I forgot about you, just like I said I wouldn't. I'll get into my Bible tonight just as soon as Dad and I get home from our drive."

❦ ❦ ❦

Back in the cart, Lucy and her dad took off down Pebbly Beach Road and watched the scuba divers off of Lover's Cove packing their gear for the night. Twilight washed the town. To the west, where they were driving, the sun sank behind the mountains. To the east, people moored their boats for the night.

Finally, they sped around Chimes Tower Road and headed toward home. They didn't say much. They didn't need to.

Normally they didn't drive past these particular streets on the way home, but it somehow looked familiar to Lucy. One block later, she realized why.

This was Jenny's street.

They drove by Jenny's small house. Lucy's heart softened and hurt at the same time.

When they got home, Lucy's mom stopped painting. "Serena called. Did they have any openings at camp next week?"

Lucy shook her head. "They don't."

"I'm sorry. Hey—how about we have our special lunch together tomorrow."

"Okay." Lucy walked upstairs. Her dad followed with the new violet.

"I'll help you find just the right place for this," he said, trailing her up the steps. They set the plant on the dresser.

"We'll water and feed it together. Keep an eye out for weeds."

"Weeds? It's inside the house!"

"Weeds can even float in through the open window. The important thing is to pluck them out as soon as you see even the littlest shoot. Otherwise they'll choke out whatever you're trying to grow."

"Okay, Dad. Thanks." Lucy kissed his cheek before he left the room. She snagged the phone and dialed Serena.

"There aren't any spaces at the camp," she told her.

"Oh no. Oh no," Serena said. "I wish we had remembered this before."

"It wouldn't have mattered," Lucy said. "They were full a long time ago. And, um, I drove by Jenny's house tonight."

"Are you still mad at her?" Serena asked.

A tear left Lucy's eye without permission and rested on her cheekbone. "I think what hurts the most is that a friend said those things about me. I shared my birthday party with her when her grandpa was sick. We had fun together. Our names were on the cake together." She let the silence hang between them before finishing.

"It hurts more when you don't expect it—from someone you thought liked you."

"I don't think she meant anything bad. I really don't. She didn't start it," Serena reminded her. "I think she likes you a lot."

Lucy sighed. "But why couldn't she just have changed whatever they said?"

"Maybe she couldn't think fast enough," Serena said. "But I saw her trying to catch your eye today when we were on the pedal boats, even though you didn't look at her. I bet she wanted to make sure everything was okay between you two."

"Maybe," Lucy said.

"I'd better go. But I wanted to tell you—I have a surprise for you tomorrow morning. Be ready at ten sharp. Okay?"

"What kind of surprise?"

"A surprise surprise. You'll see."

With that, Serena hung up the phone.

Ten o'clock sharp. Lucy smiled, a little.

As she sat down on her bed, she took her Bible out.

She opened to Matthew. "I want to read about the beginning of your life here."

After she read two chapters, she prayed. *It feels good to be with you. Thanks for everything you've given me, Jesus. I do trust you. But what's going on about this luck thing? I mean, if you look at it, things have been bad all week, even though I've been trying to do good things and help good to win.* She swallowed. *And there's two more days left this week, Lord,* she added, as if God would forget the letter's threat for the last of the five days.

Lucy saw the words *A Bevy of Blessings* printed on the bulletin saving her place in the Bible. She giggled. Why were people writing in about their backs feeling good and a brother calling home? Blessings? Lucy looked up the word *blessing* in the back of her Bible and read a few of the verses. One of them, 1 Peter 3:9, struck her heart.

Don't repay evil for evil. Don't retaliate when people say unkind things about you. Instead, pay them back with a blessing. That is what God wants you to do, and he will bless you for it.

Lucy closed her eyes. *Lord, are you asking me to pay Jenny back with a blessing—like one of the secret diary gifts?*

She knew the answer before she closed her Bible for the night. The diary girls thought the gifts would draw troubled friends together.

What blessing, Lord?

As she thought about it while getting ready for bed, Lucy glanced down at her turquoise ring and her heart stuck again. The ring Jenny had admired at the post office. The one Lucy loved.

She looked back at her Bible. Surely God wouldn't expect her to give Jenny the ring. Not when she'd already had to give up her most precious ring this week! Why, she'd be down to only one ring—her mood ring. Which was currently black.

Lucy pushed her turquoise ring on more firmly and set her alarm for 8:17 so she'd be ready for Serena's surprise.

10

Discovered!

Thursday morning . . . D Day minus one

In the morning Lucy woke before her alarm. *The fourth day.*

Will anything happen today? She sat up in bed and noticed her open Bible in the same spot she had left it the night before.

Don't repay evil for evil. Don't retaliate when people say unkind things about you. Instead, pay them back with a blessing. That is what God wants you to do, and he will bless you for it.

Lucy closed the Bible and quickly got dressed. She had to eat and do her chores before Serena arrived—with the surprise!

Serena arrived just on time.

"Well, where's my surprise?" Lucy teased.

"Patience, patience," Serena answered. "It's not something you get, it's somewhere to go."

The two of them headed up Marine Way, and as soon as they turned the corner Lucy guessed.

"Are we going to see the puppies?"

Serena just smiled.

"I thought Mrs. Marshall didn't want us over," Lucy said.

"That was yesterday. I talked to her again last night, and she said we could come."

Joy welled up inside of Lucy. *Little Venus, here I come!* "I told Claudette I would look after her pup, too, while she is in China."

Soon they pushed open the gate to Mrs. Marshall's house and arrived at the doorstep. Lucy patted the three ceramic bunnies on the step and noticed that there was a new, full bag of dog food with the supplies by Mrs. Marshall's garden.

Man alive, I should have brought some by. I'm supposed to buy the dog food. Now Mrs. Marshall had to buy some more dog food, and they're not even her dogs!

Lucy promised herself she'd bring a fresh bag next week so as not to inconvenience Mrs. Marshall, who had been so good to them.

"Good morning!" Mrs. Marshall called out as she opened the door to the girls. "Come on in."

Lucy ran over to the pups. She picked up Venus first, recognizing her by the milk splash of white on her fur, and, of course, by her Dr Pepper–colored ribbon.

"I love you, Venus," she nuzzled into the pup's neck. She held her close and then called to Serena. "Why are you standing back there?"

Serena shifted her weight on her foot. "It's your dog, not mine."

"Mama mia! What's mine is yours! Come over here." Lucy took Serena's hands, opened them, and gently deposited the little pup into her hands. "There. You love up Venus while I pet Claudette's pup."

Serena's eyes smiled warmer than her mouth even could. She nuzzled Venus while Lucy gently played with the pup with two different-colored ribbons—matching Claudette's crazy socks.

"You kids sure are good about visiting the dogs. You'll be ready for them in a couple of weeks."

Lucy thought she'd test out Mrs. Marshall, too. "I guess it was lucky for everyone that Serena and I found her, right?" Lucy pointed to the mother dog.

"Luck? Luck?" Mrs. Marshall shook her red curls. "No indeed. Mrs. Beppo needed help, you needed a puppy, and I needed some cuties to care for till I leave in August. How can that be luck? God arranged it all just so."

Lucy slowly nodded her agreement. It made sense and her heart responded. But if it wasn't bad luck, then what was going on with her life? Why hadn't Katie responded? And what would the next two days hold?

After staying just long enough to love the puppies but not wear them out, the girls left.

"Wanna do something this afternoon?" Serena asked. "Beach?"

"No, I'm . . . ah, having lunch with my mom."

"Oh, that's nice. I guess I'll go home and do something with Abuela. She's leaving tomorrow."

"You must be glad."

Serena didn't answer right away. "I don't know."

They arrived at Lucy's house, and her mom was in the kitchen. Baking.

Here was something new.

Normally Mom would do egg salad or peanut butter or something. Nothing that involved an oven, though. Oh no.

"What are you doing?" Lucy asked.

"I wanted our picnic to be fun. Is a picnic okay?" Mom reached a potholder into the oven. Even before they came out of the oven, Lucy knew the cookies were burnt—she smelled burnt chocolate chips. Mom seemed distracted, preoccupied.

"Oh dear. I'd better try again." She stared straight at the oven, though, and not at Lucy.

"No, Mom, it's okay. I like them well done." *And I only have to eat one if there's other stuff.*

"No, no, I want to make another batch. Why don't you go upstairs for a few minutes and I'll call you? Okay?"

"Okay." Lucy smiled as she headed toward the computer. She remembered Mom saying, *"I try hard. I really do."*

"Okay."

She logged on to check her email.

An email from Katie! Finally! And it said, *Re: Chain Letter.*

But when Lucy opened it, the letters were all scrambled and she couldn't understand anything at all! Lucy picked up the phone and dialed her cousin. Enough was enough.

Five rings and then voice mail.

"Katie, this is Lucy. I can't read your email. Call me back pronto, okay?"

She hung up and walked upstairs. When she got there, she saw that her mom had straightened her room.

Sweet.

Then Lucy noticed something on the desk, something dusty . . . a balled-up piece of paper.

Lucy's stomach fell. She leaned over and looked under her bed. It had been swept clean.

Her eyes looked at the ball again. Inside, she knew, sat all the angry words and thoughts of a few days ago.

Oh no.

Had her mother simply set the ball there while she cleaned, or had she opened it and read to see if it was worth saving?

Mystery Call

Thursday afternoon . . .

Lucy stared at the balled-up paper. Was that why Mom had seemed upset downstairs? Lucy would have to talk with her about being mad about the ring now, no matter what.

She walked downstairs. Her mom was in the process of carrying the picnic outside.

"Can I help?" Lucy asked.

"Yes," her mother answered. "Can you carry these?"

Lucy smiled. Egg salad sandwiches. Of course. She took the platter and walked out back with her mother. Mom had already put a blanket down on the grass under one of the trees, near the star-shaped jasmine bush.

"Just set the sandwiches down here, and I'll put the veggies next to them," her mom said.

Lucy did as she was told. The two of them went back into the house to get ice water, napkins, and the fresh batch of cookies.

Once settled on the blanket, Lucy's mom relaxed and breathed out a long sigh. "Well." She smiled. "I feel much better now."

Lucy tiptoed into the conversation. "Is there anything you're upset about?"

Mom grinned. "Not anymore. Now that I got everything together and out here, I feel better. I really wanted everything to be special for us, you know, and I'm not a big party person."

A dry eucalyptus leaf fluttered down and landed between them.

"Thanks for cleaning my room," Lucy started. "You sure didn't have to sweep out under my bed." She held her breath.

"Oh, never mind," her mother said. "I noticed dad had the sniffles some nights and thought I'd better dust under the furniture. Dust troubles his sinuses. I decided I'd get under yours, too. I found a couple of things under there and left them on your desk."

So she hadn't read the letter after all. Now Lucy wouldn't have to tell her anything. But she was still mad about the opal ring.

Mom picked some of the wild daisies in the grass and tried to weave them together. "Ever since I saw that cute ring of daisies that Serena wove for you a few weeks back, I've been wanting one for myself," she said.

Lucy picked some and tried to weave the daisies, too. Every time she'd string a few together, the whole thing would fall apart. "I can't do it, either," she giggled.

"I guess we'll just have to settle for sticking some in our

hair." Mom stuck one in her blond hair, where it hung crookedly over her ear. Lucy was going to tell her but decided it was so cute she'd just let it go. Lucy stuck one in her own hair, too.

They ate the sandwiches. Lucy folded up her napkin—unusually neat. "I want to tell you something." Lucy put her chin on her knees. "I was really mad at you when you took Grandma Anne's ring back. I understand your reasons and everything, but I felt like, well, you should have thought of that before."

Mom's eyes misted over. "I handled that badly. I just panicked over losing the ring, and then I didn't want to have anything bad happen to it while you were responsible, so you wouldn't feel bad later, too. I didn't think it through very well. I'm sorry. Will you forgive me?"

"Yes," Lucy said, letting go of it in her heart. And as soon as she did, the bad feeling inside her blew away, too.

"It hasn't been an easy week for you, has it?" Mom said. "Here, have another cookie. Aren't they good?"

"Uh, I'm full," Lucy said. "It *has* been kind of a hard week. So you really don't believe in luck? You know, good luck and bad luck?"

"Hmm. Do you feel like you've been having bad luck this week?"

"Well, a lot of bad things have happened. First the ring got lost, and then you took it away. And someone said something really mean to me at the beach. And now everyone's going to camp, and there's no room for me." *Things didn't go as I planned with the housekeeper's gift or Claudette's, either.*

"Has anything good happened this week?"

Lucy pulled a stem of grass from the area just beside the blanket and stuck the fresh white root into her mouth. "We had a great trip to the *Queen Mary* with Serena. I got to see Venus. Dad and I had a good time last night."

"So was that good luck then?"

Lucy smiled. "I don't know. I guess it was just kind of . . . life." She pulled the chewed-up grass out of her mouth and tossed it to the side of the blanket.

"Life is a mix of good and bad," her mother said.

Lucy chewed the stem and thought. Dad had said there wasn't luck but practice. Mom had said it was the Lord who rewards. Mrs. Marshall said God arranged all things. In the Bible, God himself said He blessed.

Lucy wanted to believe, but she struggled. She just hadn't seen any rewards or blessings. But the truth was the truth.

"I guess if there really was good luck and bad luck, then God wouldn't be in control, would He?"

Mom ruffled Lucy's hair. "I think you have a lot to teach me, young lady."

They each shook out their hair and let the daisies tumble to the ground.

"I've got to do some things downtown," her mother said as she headed into the house. Lucy brought in the dishes, picked a blossom off of the jasmine bush, and then went up to her room.

Lucy sat on her bed, not moving for a minute. "Okay." Finally, Lucy took off her turquoise ring and looked at it, inside and out. She remembered the plump Navajo grandmother bending over to place the ring on Lucy's finger. Then Lucy polished the ring with a little gray cloth she kept in her secret drawer for just that purpose. The silver shone like moonlight; the triangle stone was river blue, a color she'd never seen anywhere else.

Then Lucy sat down with a piece of paper. She was going to have to forgive Jenny if she was going to do this. *Please help me to forgive her, God. I don't feel like it right now.*

As she closed her eyes and sat there for a moment, Lucy remembered laughing with Jenny as the two of them danced the Sprinkler at their mutual birthday party three weeks earlier. They had looked so goofy.

Lucy opened her eyes and giggled. She reached over and took one of the jasmine blossoms and one by one picked off the few petals, gathering them in the hollow of her hand. "I forgive you, Jenny," she whispered, and then blew the petals into the air.

Lucy wrapped the ring in Kleenex and put it, with the other jasmine blossom, into a padded envelope. She put a short note in with it. *I like you. A lot. If you want to, pass the blessing on.*

She sealed the envelope, wrote Jenny's address on it, stuck five stamps on it—just to make sure—and put the letter in her canvas sack.

She looked at the calendar on her desk. A giant "D" was drawn on tomorrow's date. The final day.

Mom came out of her room, her own bag swinging on her shoulder. Lucy met her in the hall.

"Do you mind if I go with you to mail this?" Lucy asked.

"All right." Her mother looked strange. "But you go your way at the post office, and I'll go mine. I'll meet you at home." They left the house, and a few blocks later Mom hurried off, turning the corner. Lucy walked into the post office. Her hand didn't want to let go of the letter. What it really wanted to do was to rip the ring out of the envelope, put it back on her finger, and go to the pharmacy to buy something else for Jenny. Another ring, maybe, or some earrings. But Lucy knew that's not what she was supposed to do.

"Pluck the weeds before they choke out what you're trying to grow," Dad had said. Lucy pulled down the lid and dropped the envelope in. Then she let the lid clang shut. The lid said the mail wouldn't be picked up again till Friday—tomorrow. But Jenny would get the ring on Saturday anyway, before she left to go to camp with the others.

Lucy walked home.

Jesus, tomorrow is D Day. This has been an awful week. You can see how someone would believe it was bad luck if they wanted to. Right? I do believe what I said—that you're in charge. But I'm wondering, God, and I hope you won't be mad because I'm asking. Is it really true about the rewards for doing the right things, and your blessings, too?

After she got home, Lucy cleaned the kitchen a bit. Then the phone rang.

"Hello?"

It was a man with a deep voice. "May I speak with Victoria Larson?"

"She's not here. May I take a message?"

"No thanks. I'll call back in a few minutes." The man clicked off before Lucy could say another word.

Weird.

Ten minutes later Mom arrived. "Did anyone call?" she asked.

"Yeah." Lucy turned. "A man. He asked for you."

Lucy's mother looked troubled. "Did he leave his name?"

"No. He said he'd call back."

The phone rang again. Mom dashed to get it, and as she did so, firmly closed the kitchen door between Lucy and herself.

Open Immediately

Friday morning . . . D Day!

The final day was here.

Lucy kept herself busy during the morning. Her mother never did tell her who had been on the phone, and Mom kept secrets well.

"Don't forget Serena's coming over in a few hours," Lucy reminded her mother as the two of them folded towels. "We're going to finish reading the old diary. And write in our own."

"I haven't forgotten," her mom said. "But I have a few errands to do first. Will you be okay alone?"

"Why don't I come with you?" Lucy asked. "It will give me something to kill the time."

"No thanks," her mom said. She got her purse and left.

Lucy decided she would head to town anyway and get some fresh Jelly Bellies. She was starting to worry about Katie, too. Strange email—and no return call. For her final good deed, Lucy wrote a funny little letter and decided to send it to Katie so she would get something *good* in the mail. What Katie really needed was God. Lucy's stomach felt a little weird. She hadn't told Katie that she'd been spending time with God again. It just hadn't come up.

Lucy wrote at the end of the letter: *This is a cool formula, kind of like the one on the chain letter, but only the good part. 1 Cross + 3 Nails = 4given. You're the best cousin ever. More later, gator. XOXO Lucy.* She sealed the letter. It wasn't really secret, not from Katie. But it was a good deed.

She'd head to the post office to mail it, but first Lucy wanted to stop by Sweet Dreams. Maybe Jake would be working today.

She combed her hair and slipped in a pair of jeweled clips. After taking her bag and then locking the front door behind her, Lucy set off.

The day did not disappoint. Jake was working.

"Hi, Dr Pepper!"

"Hi, Jake," she answered.

"Jelly Bellies?" he asked, already heading over to the scoop.

"Of course." Lucy smiled.

Jake went around the counter and showed her to the back wall. "These are all really fresh, because I'm bringing some to camp next week. Are you coming?"

Lucy's heart sank. "No. They're full."

"I'm sorry," Jake said. "I wish you were going."

Lucy smiled and paid. When Jake turned his back to help the next customer, Lucy slipped a quarter into the tip jar.

She headed toward the post office and mailed Katie's letter. *I might as well get the mail.* She slipped the key into the post office box, grabbed the mail, quickly looked through it, and stuck it into her canvas sack.

On the way home she noticed the pet store was having a sale on dog food. She grabbed a bag and stopped over at Mrs. Marshall's. The ceramic bunnies were glad to see her. They met Lucy with the same bright eyes and cheerful smile as always.

Mrs. Marshall answered the door. "I wasn't expecting you," she said, her red hair nighttime fuzzy.

"I'm not staying," Lucy explained. "I just wanted to bring some dog food—so you don't run out."

"Well, aren't you girls nice," Mrs. Marshall said. "Just two days ago your friend Serena sneaked into the yard and brought a bag of dog food, too. Didn't knock or anything—probably didn't want to disturb me. You can set your bag over there by the one she brought." Mrs. Marshall pointed to the supply area.

Lucy carried the dog food over and set it next to Serena's. Then she noticed something she hadn't noticed yesterday. A jasmine blossom rested on the bag Serena had snuck in. Serena must have given her secret gift the day Mrs. Marshall had had a bad day.

Lucy looked at her watch. It was nearly time for Serena to meet her at home. As she raced toward home, where her mom and her friend would meet her, Lucy thought maybe she hadn't counted the real rewards and blessings. Maybe she'd seen them but hadn't realized—like not realizing the dog food was from Serena. And she loved getting closer to her mom. Then there was a trip this week with her best friend, and all the people who wished she were going to camp with them. Lucy grinned at herself, remembering making fun of the Bevy of Blessings in the bulletin. *Kind of like blessings of phone calls from brothers and no back pain!*

Lucy hurried home, pushed open the squeaky screen, and tossed the mail on the table in the front hallway. "Hi, Mom!" She headed toward the kitchen for a snack. *Something cool. Maybe a Popsicle.*

"Lucy?" her mother called. "Did you look through this mail?"

"Yes."

Her mother came into the kitchen and held up a letter. "Did you see this one addressed to you?"

Lucy closed the freezer and took the letter from her mother's hand. Sure enough, it was addressed to Miss Lucy Larson. It must have slid inside a magazine or something and Lucy hadn't seen it. The words *Open Immediately!* were written on the side of the envelope—nearly like the word *Urgent!* had been written on the chain letter almost a week before.

Oh no. This *was* the final day.

But this time the return address was from Catalina Island. The address was typed out—clearly an adult, not a child, had sent this.

"Do you know what it is?" she asked her mother.

"Nope," Mom answered. "But I'm curious. Aren't you?"

"Yes!" Lucy slipped her finger under the back of the envelope, ripping it open before pulling out a single, professional-looking folded letter.

Who Knew?

Friday afternoon . . .

Dear Miss Larson and Parents, it began.

> *We have one opening at camp this coming week. One of our campers is, at the last moment, unable to attend. She asked that we offer you her slot and deposit before making it generally available. Please have a parent call this number right away and ask for camp director Jim Rice. We were given only your address and not your phone number, but time is of the essence. Because camp will begin so shortly, we will offer the slot to someone else if I don't hear from you immediately. Sincerely, Mr. Jim Rice.*

Lucy couldn't believe it! She dropped the letter on the counter and grabbed her mother's hand. "I get to go! I get to go to camp! Way to go, Rachel!"

"Maybe," her mother said. "If the slot is not taken."

Lucy couldn't help thinking that, if the slot was taken,

it would be the ultimate bad luck of the whole week.

No, she reminded herself. *There is no such thing as luck.*

Mom picked up the phone. "I'll call Mr. Rice."

Lucy practically hung over her mom's shoulder. "Yes, Mr. Rice, this is Victoria Larson, Lucy's mother. Please call us back at 3578 regarding camp next week."

After her mother left the voice mail, she said, "I wonder how much it costs. We spent a lot of money on the *Queen Mary* this week."

"It can't be too much," Lucy said. "All my friends are going."

"All of your friends had a year to plan ahead for it," Mom answered. "We'll see how much—and if the slot is still open—when Mr. Rice calls back."

A flutter of fear ran through Lucy. She peeked out the front window. No Serena yet.

She dialed Rachel, who answered the phone.

"Rachel? It's Lucy. Thanks for the camp slot!"

There was silence at the other end, and then Rachel said, "What?"

"The opening at camp. Didn't you tell them to call you if there was an opening? Well, today I got a letter from Mr. Jim Rice saying there was an opening, and . . . uh, I was sure you had asked them to offer it to me."

"Jim Rice is the director, but he didn't call me. But if he says there's an opening, I'm sure there is. Terrific! Lucy, I'll see you there."

"Okay," Lucy said. She hung the phone back on the hook.

If it wasn't Rachel, who was it? And *was* Mr. Rice still

holding the slot open for Lucy?

The phone rang and Lucy ran to answer it. "Hello?"

"It's Katie."

"Oh. Hey, cous! Your email was totally unreadable. What's going on?"

"My computer crashed," Katie said. "I didn't even get email for days, and then I couldn't read anything or write anything. Now it's sending out garbage."

"So," Lucy said. "Did you have good luck with your chain letter?"

"Not really," Katie finally admitted. "My computer crashed. I got a bad haircut."

"*Nothing* good happened?"

"Well, I got first place on the swim team. But I'd been practicing for a month." Katie cleared her throat. "Did you send the letter out?"

"No," Lucy admitted.

"I should have known you'd be too smart to do that." Katie sounded so sad. Lucy was glad she'd sent the funny letter to her.

"Ha!" Lucy said. "I had the thing copied and ready to go. Then one of my friends told me *she* wouldn't want a letter like that, so I decided not to send it."

"Nothing bad happened?"

"Just normal life," Lucy said. "Good and bad." A few minutes later they hung up.

Katie's call—and Katie's normal week, with good and bad life-things happening—was one more answer to the question of luck.

Lucy would have faith that camp would work out.

Mr. Rice would certainly call back soon.

A knock at the door interrupted Lucy's thoughts. She ran to open it and found Serena there, yellow umbrella in hand.

"It's starting to rain," Serena said. "Should we skip the beach?"

Lucy nodded. "Let's set the umbrella up outside. The blanket is still on the ground from our picnic yesterday."

Before they went outside, Serena set down a plastic container on the counter. "For your family."

"What is it?" Lucy asked.

"Mexican stew," Serena said. She blushed. "I made it with Abuela. With, um—" she cleared her throat—"avocado leaves."

Lucy held back a smile. Avocado leaves for Abuela, dog food for Mrs. Marshall. Sweet Serena.

They went outside and propped the umbrella open against the eucalyptus tree to shelter them from the tiny drops.

"Best news!"

"What?"

"I might get to go to camp after all!"

Serena grabbed Lucy's hands and they screamed together. "No! How did you get a spot?"

Lucy explained about her mom's call to Mr. Rice and then showed the letter to Serena. "Someone requested that I get her spot and deposit. Who could it be?"

Serena sat there for a minute and then smiled. "Well, I couldn't say for sure, but I saw Jenny at the ferry terminal today. My family was bringing Abuela to go home, and

Jenny was there with her mom and her grandpa. She told me they were going to a family reunion this week in San Diego. They hadn't planned on it, but her grandpa's not doing so well so they decided to have it now."

Lucy closed her eyes. *Jenny.* Maybe Jenny had received the ring from Lucy and wanted to do something nice back.

Lucy's eyes opened when she realized the ring wouldn't even be delivered to Jenny's P.O. Box till today, and the letter was mailed yesterday! So Jenny couldn't have known. She wouldn't have even received the ring yet!

"When did they know they had to go?"

"Wednesday night, I think. I don't know." Serena smiled. "I *told* you Jenny likes you. She was trying to catch your eye at the pedal boats when we were talking about camp, but they had to return theirs before we did."

Oh, Jenny. I'm sorry. Suddenly Lucy was so glad she had obeyed what she felt the Lord had told her to do and sent the ring to Jenny.

"I hope the space is still open," Serena said. She squeezed Lucy's hand. "You want to read the diary now or tell our secret deeds?"

"Will you weave a daisy headband while I read the diary?" Lucy opened up the diary while Serena started to weave a flower chain out of the misty-eyed wild daisies.

"I'm afraid it's going to get wet," Serena said as Lucy found their page.

"Let's go to my room, then," Lucy said.

Serena quickly wove the flower circle and tossed it onto Lucy's hair. Then they grabbed their gear and ran into the house.

"The flowers aren't for me, but thanks!" Once in her room, the girls settled on Lucy's bed.

I wish the phone would ring.

Lucy set the new diary on her dresser so it would be just the two of them with the old diary on her bed.

"Come on!" Serena said.

Lucy opened to Serena's great-grandmother's blocky handwriting. "You go first."

Serena took the book and began to read aloud.

"Well, Diary, this has been a week indeed. We all had such great fun with the secret gifts. mary got a poem and a small box of chocolates. We all know she loves sweets!"

The handwriting changed, so Lucy began reading.

"Serena got a silver hairbrush, something she's long wanted. I think I know who it's from, but I'll never tell. Once the girls saw everyone getting and giving with love, we all softened up. We never did find out who broke the vase, but accidents happen. Trudy's mother said she'd always hated that old vase and now could buy another one. Then Trudy suggested we not ever tell each other who gave the gifts, keeping it secret from all but the Lord, who sees everything. I'm not even telling Serena what I gave the others, although of course she knows what I've received!"

The people we gave gifts to may never know they were from us. But we did good things, and it made a difference and will keep making a difference in people's lives as they pass on good things. The best news—we are all pals again.

Serena smiled as Lucy handed the diary back to her.

"Next week, though, we won't be able to keep the secret. Mary and I are going to do something that absolutely everyone will notice."

Lucy leaned over and read the remaining words.

"If our fathers agree, that is. They are not keen on anything that seems like we're becoming daring and modern. But we know our onions, and this is absolutely it! Till next week, Diary, we remain,
faithful friends."

"Should we write in our diary now?" Serena asked. "And should we keep our good deeds secret, too? Like the diary girls?"

"Sure." Lucy thought back to the housekeeper and Betsy. Even if they never knew who gave them the gifts, God would. And Lucy had brought them happiness.

So Serena scribbled in their diary about how much

better she felt holding her tongue. When she did, she got to know and love—and cook with—Roberto's abuela.

"Abuela gave me some silver-tipped painting brushes," Serena said. "She had them shipped from Mexico just for me. I didn't even know she knew how to FedEx!"

Serena drew a picture of the brushes in the book. Lucy giggled and wrote in about her week.

> *I learned how to look at little things as blessings and rewards. Also, life has both good and bad. You can't always figure it out.*

Lucy shook the pen so the ink would flow again.

> *But it's not luck. A lot of times we have choices in how things work out. No matter what, God is in control.*

She drew a picture of a stick with a marshmallow on it. "Camp stuff," she said, smiling, hopeful she'd be going. They signed off, *Serena and Lucy, Faithful Friends*.

Finally, the Faithful Friends plucked two jasmine blossoms from the front vine—one for each of them—twined them together, and pressed them into their diary forever.

Just as she closed the diary, the phone rang. Lucy jumped up and ran into her mother's room.

It wasn't really eavesdropping if her mother knew she was there, right?

"Yes, Mr. Rice. Yes, that's fine," her mom said. "And the cost?"

Lucy held her breath and then released it like a slow leak in a bicycle tire.

"No, I'm sure that will be fine. We'll look forward to seeing you then. Good-bye!"

"So I can go?"

"You can go."

Lucy jumped up and down and ran to her room singing, "Hi-ho, hi-ho, it's off to camp we go!" *Thank you, God! For big rewards sometimes, too!*

Lucy and Serena celebrated and planned, and then Serena packed up and left.

"Lucy!" Her mom called to her from the top of the stairs.

Lucy turned back around. "Yes?"

"I have something for you."

Lucy walked upstairs, into her room, where her mom was waiting.

Mom held out a small blue box with floral etching on top. Lucy took it from her. She slowly opened the blue box and gasped when she saw what was inside.

The opal ring.

Her eyes opened wide, and she looked at her mother. "Shall I just keep it in the box till I'm big enough?"

"Try it on," her mom suggested.

Lucy slipped it on her fourth finger, the finger where the turquoise ring used to live. It fit perfectly.

Lucy opened her eyes in wonder. "What happened? It fits!"

Mom looked at her. "I told you I had to keep it because it was too big. Well, yesterday, after our picnic, I had a new thought. You really are growing up, and the way you handled this week proves it. So it's not that *you* had to get bigger. The ring just needed to be made smaller."

Lucy smiled. "Oh, Mom!"

"So," Mom continued, "I took it to a jeweler in town to see if he could size it. He called yesterday to say he could, and it would be ready this morning."

The mysterious caller, Lucy remembered.

"If it's too big or small, he can adjust it. You can wear it when you want to or keep it in the box if you're worried about losing it. It's your choice."

Lucy hugged her mom, who hugged her back.

"All right, all right, I've got work to do," Mom said. She never did like too much emotion. She was probably way over her limit this week.

As her mom stood up to leave, Lucy placed the flower circle on her mom's head. "I wanted to give you an even bigger gift this week, but at least I can give this to you. Serena had to make it, of course."

They laughed together.

"This is a lovely thought, a lovely blessing," her mom said.

After her mother left the room, Lucy touched the top of the blue jewelry box. It didn't just have any flower etching on top; it was an etching of the island's jasmine flower!

Jasmine. Our special flower for giving secret gifts.

"Who knew?" she whispered, knowing the answer as she spoke the question.

God knew.

"Thank you, Lord," Lucy whispered as she ran her finger over her opal ring. "For everything. I love being more like you, passing every good thing on to others."

But I know!
I, the Lord, search all hearts
and examine secret motives.
I give all people their due rewards,
according to what their actions deserve.

JEREMIAH 17:10

SANDRA BYRD and her family really did eat a grand meal on the *Queen Mary*—though pheasant wasn't served that day (and she would have tried it if it had been!). Forget the *Titanic*—the *Queen Mary* is still afloat! The boat is the coolest ship, a totally different kind of hotel and the most amazing back-in-time trip around.

Sandra lives near beautiful Seattle, between snow-capped Mount Rainier and the Space Needle, with her husband and two children (and let's not forget her new puppy, Duchess). When she's not writing, she's usually reading, but she also likes to scrapbook, listen to music, and spend time with friends. Besides writing THE HIDDEN DIARY books, she's also the author of the bestselling series SECRET SISTERS.

For more information on THE HIDDEN DIARY series, visit Sandra's Web site: *www.sandrabyrd.com*. Or you can write to Sandra at

Sandra Byrd
P.O. Box 1207
Maple Valley, WA 98038

**Don't miss book six
of THE HIDDEN DIARY,
Change of Heart!**

For a preview of Lucy and Serena's next diary adventure, just hold up this page in front of a mirror.

Lucy and Serena get to camp—with more excitement than they bargained for! When Lucy accidentally discovers a camper's tightly held secret, she's forced to make a decision in which there are no safe choices.

GO for the GOLD

With Beverly Lewis!

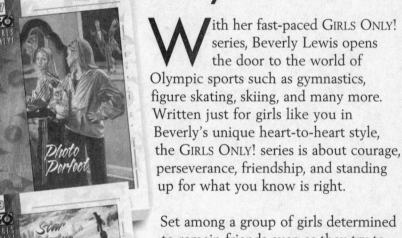

With her fast-paced GIRLS ONLY! series, Beverly Lewis opens the door to the world of Olympic sports such as gymnastics, figure skating, skiing, and many more. Written just for girls like you in Beverly's unique heart-to-heart style, the GIRLS ONLY! series is about courage, perseverance, friendship, and standing up for what you know is right.

Set among a group of girls determined to remain friends even as they try to balance practice, school, and competition, each GIRLS ONLY book will bring you deeper into their hearts and dreams. Join them on their quests for success.

1. *Dreams on Ice*
2. *Only the Best*
3. *A Perfect Match*
4. *Reach for the Stars*
5. *Follow the Dream*
6. *Better Than Best*
7. *Photo Perfect*
8. *Star Status*

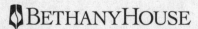

BETHANYHOUSE

11400 Hampshire Avenue S. • Minneapolis, MN 55438
(800) 328-6109 • www.bethanyhouse.com